As It Pleases The King

As it Pleases the King
Copyright © 2020
Sara Harris

ISBN: 978-1-952474-10-1

Cover concept and design by David Warren.

Published by WordCrafts Press
Cody, Wyoming 82414
www.wordcrafts.net

THE KING'S PLEASURE SERIES
BOOK I

As It Pleases The King

SARA HARRIS

WordCrafts

Sometimes

We must chase our happiness like our lives depend on it. And more often than not, it does.

To Wesley.
Thanks for being my happy ever after.

T HROCKENHOLT P RIORY
Lincolnshire—February 1542

"England is again set to be without a queen?" The news gave me pause as the words rolled slowly off my tongue. The potato I'd been scrubbing dangled precariously over the pail of water that had been clear hours before. Despite the water having grown thick and brown, the giant sack on the floor was still half full.

My cousin Elizabeth glanced at me over her own steaming bucket, her cheeks rosy. Normally she would fret if asked to help with any preparations for guests, especially scrubbing the floors, as if her dollop of royal blood forced her to rely only on our few attendants. Even if it would be quicker to just do it herself. But not today. "Mother told me the truth circles about Court like flies over a corpse. Queen Catherine hasn't uttered one *word* to prove her innocence!"

"So she will be executed then, just like Anne Boleyn. Suppose this one will request a French swordsman as well?" The harshness of my words struck me. This was a woman's life hanging in the balance. I let the potato sink into the murky water and did the sign of the cross.

In nominae Patris et Filii et Spiritus Sancti.

Mother died soon after my birth eighteen years ago, but still I preserved her faith in my heart despite the growing popularity of Protestantism. I fished out the potato and set it atop the mountain of those I'd already scoured. "Perhaps the King will choose a good Catholic girl to marry next to bring England back to the True Faith."

Elizabeth dipped her rag in the bucket and dropped to her knees. "Perhaps he will. A good Catholic girl. Or perhaps not. No doubt she will be younger than Catherine Howard, and fairer too." She paused in her scrubbing and arched an eyebrow at me. "Perhaps His Majesty is already sending out his groomsmen to scour the English countryside in search of his next bride, having found none abroad?"

I gathered a fresh armload of potatoes and dropped them into my bucket. Dirty water splashed onto Elizabeth's clean floor.

"Bridget!" she scolded. "Mother said we are to help prepare for supper this evening. *And clean.* Getting ready for this royal visit is too much for our servants to handle on their own."

I giggled. "I *am* helping prepare supper, Cousin. You tend to your floor."

Elizabeth snuffed and plopped her rag over the dirty potato water.

As our giggles died off, I glanced down at her. "You don't suppose our guests tonight are coming here on the *King's* bidding?" I shook my head at the sheer idiocy of noble groomsmen coming to our home in Lincolnshire in a futile attempt to sniff out the future Queen of England. "Truly I tell you, I pity any poor girl that His Majesty takes to wife. Really. Even if she be a Reformer."

Elizabeth shrugged. Her white hood shifted over her blonde hair as she scrubbed. "You mean to say you would choose *not* to be Queen, should His Majesty choose you, out of all the maids in England?"

"Elizabeth, really!" My jaw went slack. "Queen Catherine, that as she was, is set to be *executed.* Can you not see how they all wind up? Even if His Majesty chose a good Catholic girl, I fear she would wind up a head shorter—or be shoved off to die alone in a faraway castle. Like his true Spanish wife, Catherine of Aragon."

Elizabeth's musical laugh tinkled along the stone floor. Each stone, all of them with a bloody past, was dug from the nearby Trent River and carried up to this very farmhouse before being laid by the monks who lived here, back when our home was still Throckenholt Priory. Before His Majesty dissolved the monasteries, burned the monks, and gifted the priory and all its lands to my aunt, Lady Denny.

"I suppose Mother could tell it best, what it is really like in the Queen's Chambers, since she is a maid to Queen Catherine." Elizabeth sat back and dragged her hand across her brow. "You don't suppose Mother..." She squelched her words and shook her head. "No, it's too absurd a thought."

I hefted the filthy bucket of water to my chest and trudged to the servant's door. I dumped it unceremoniously onto the frozen ground. Elizabeth needn't have finished her sentence. The same question plagued my mind. *Could Lady Denny have arranged this dinner so my cousin or myself might become the next wife of Henry VIII? Or perhaps even—I gulped. The next Queen of England?*

Candles lit the stone dining hall of Throckenholt Priory to a warm glow. I mustered every manner I'd ever been taught as I sat straight backed in my chair and tried not to look at Elizabeth, whose mischievous smile had danced across her lips all through dinner. She had cinched my whalebone corset tighter than normal, thus making this entire dinner affair even more uncomfortable.

I tried not to look at the two courtiers who filled the seats on either side of me, dressed in their fancy velvet doublets, but they looked at me. I caught their glassy eyes roving over the blue velvet that clung to my curves. The fabric hung dreadfully low, lower than I thought necessary, but Lady Denny had been insistent that we reveal *just a bit more*. Both men drummed the French lace tablecloth, and their gold-encased jewels squeezed their fat fingers like sausages.

Elizabeth however had no qualms with dressing to impress. Her smooth black damask gown didn't leave much to the courtiers' imaginations, as evident in their lusty gazes at her voluminous chest.

All evening, through heaping platters of black pudding and marzipan, I laughed when I was expected to laugh, sipped the royal wine the courtiers brought when I was expected to sip, and nibbled bits of roasted beaver tail and boiled potatoes when I was expected to nibble as Lady Denny lorded over us silently from the far end of the immaculate table.

I tried to pay attention to my plate and draw none unto myself. After the spice cake was reduced to crumbs and the last of the wine was drunk, the courtiers pushed back from the table in unison. Elizabeth and I stood, followed by Lady Denny, whose face was severe, but somewhat less pinched than it was during dinner.

The two men shared a look before the pudgier one with the white plume in his hat spoke. "I believe we shall retire till morning."

The other, with a voice much higher pitched than the first, interrupted him. "At which time both young ladies, Lady Elizabeth and Lady Bridget, shall accompany us back to Court." He stuck his thumbs in the waist of his matching velvet chauses that stretched tight across his bulging waistline. "Both have satisfactorily met the *minimal* requirements issued by His Majesty including grace, dignity, and feminine beauty. And, of course, a royal bloodline." They shared a quiet cackle.

Elizabeth dipped into a deep curtsy as my jaw fell open. Remembering myself, I followed my cousin's lead and dipped down in a bow.

"Thank you, sirs," I muttered through trembling lips. Something knotted in my stomach and fell like cold stones in a pot of three-day old soup. It wasn't the beaver tail or the artichoke stew that brought the green hue to the world before me. It was fear.

Tower Green Scaffold
February 13, 1542

I stood beside Elizabeth. The new emerald green shoes I'd been given by my attending maids crunched in the thin layer of frost that covered the ground. Earlier in my dressing suite, one of the servants whispered that the color matched that of my eyes. I wasn't sure I believed her.

The newly risen sun did little to brighten the overcast sky that cloaked the scaffold on the Tower Green.

"Never before have I seen so many people in one place," Elizabeth mused. "And here we are, in the front row to the Queen of England's execution."

The fancy breakfast of quail's eggs and French toast soured in my stomach as Elizabeth chattered on, almost giddy. "Surely this woman is the most hated of all His Majesty's queens."

Knots pushed burning bile into my throat. Still, Elizabeth continued. "It has been widely whispered that even her own uncle, the Duke of Norfolk, now despises her. He calls her, among many other things, a *common prostitute.*"

Thankfully several people pushed between us, bound for the scaffold, and saved me from having to respond to my cousin. Like a leaf fighting the current of a rushing river, I struggled not to be picked up and carried along with them. The lace-trimmed handkerchief I'd been given was lost in the process.

"Drat!" I yanked off my gloves and dropped to my knees. Feverishly, I patted the trampled ground to no avail. Frozen twigs and grass poked my hands mercilessly as I peered through the exquisitely shod feet of those who were also privy to the royal execution. However, none stooped to lend a hand in my futile search.

A husky voice, slightly French, met my ears. "M'lady."

I glanced upward. A leather-clad man stared back at me, my handkerchief dangling helplessly in his grasp. His eyes bore down on me with an almost tangible weight.

I accepted the lacy fabric with trembling hands. Our skin brushed, and fire trailed from his fingertips and sizzled where our skin met.

Something stormy in his eyes, cold and steely blue, took my breath and tightened my chest. "T-thank you, m'lord."

Black locks curled across his forehead, and the hint of stubble shadowed his angular features giving him a mystical look. He stared at me hard, so hard that it took every ounce of willpower I possessed not to crawl between the fancy feet of those around me just to escape it.

After what seemed an eternity, he spoke again. "Miss, I am no one's lord."

I winced at the harshness spat forth with his words.

The mysterious man in brown turned on his booted heel and disappeared so quickly I wondered if I actually conversed with him at all. Elizabeth knelt at my side and grasped my elbow. With her help, I found my way back onto my feet.

Her eyes widened as we squeezed back into our place on the front row. "Cousin! What *ever* were you doing, groveling in the dirt?"

"Someone bumped me, and I lost my handkerchief," I sputtered. The man in brown reappeared, squelching my words.

It was real.

His slick black head broke the surface of the audience as he trotted easily up the scaffold steps. His brown leather riding boots scraped together in an odd tune. My heart quickened to a racing pace as I watched him.

He knelt, his back to me, before a fat man in purple stepped to the forefront of the scaffold stage and readied the block. In doing so, he effectively blocked my view. My palms felt cold and wet inside my gloves.

Probably from patting the ice, I told myself. Still, I sensed a change.

"Bridget?" Elizabeth's voice was insistent in my ear. "Bridget!"

Like an ocean wave, silence crashed down upon the monstrous crowd as it parted on some unspoken cue, making way for a solitary man. Behind him trailed two women. The first, cloaked in a dark velvet cape that trailed the icy ground behind her. The second, clad in only a simple white robe, which billowed a bit as she walked. The woman in white hugged her arms across her chest and glanced about, like a mad dog, through empty eyes.

Slowly, the unlikely trio made their way effortlessly through the silent crowd and ascended the tumbledown stairs.

"They are executing Lady Rochford first," I breathed as the figure in white, the doomed Jane Boleyn, stepped toward the chopping block. Forgetting the odd emotions that moments before had overtaken my body, I dropped my voice low so only my cousin could hear. "Do you believe what they say, that Lady Jane gave information to Master Cromwell, which in turn led to her husband George's beheading?"

"Surely she did," Elizabeth whispered back. "I know her sis-ter-in-law, Anne Boleyn, was a light young woman, but I don't believe she was involved in an incestuous relationship with her own brother." She glanced at me and pulled her cloak tighter against the chill. "Do you?"

I opened my mouth, but so did Lady Jane. I closed mine to listen.

"Good Christian people, I come hither to die. But I do so with complete and utter faith and trust in God, whom I have committed many sins against from my youth upwards." With a jump, she paused and glanced back as though someone had tapped her shoulder. However, nobody had.

Visibly shaken, Lady Rochford continued. "I have offended the king's royal Majesty very dangerously, so my punishment today is just and deserved. I am justly condemned by the laws of this realm and by Parliament."

Elizabeth leaned close. "Will she cry?"

I ignored her.

The tremble in the voice of the condemned grew louder. "All of you who watch me die should learn from my example and change your own lives. You must gladly obey the king in all things, for he is a just and godly prince. I pray for his preservation and beseech you all to do the same. I now entrust my soul to God and pray for his mercy."

She paused once more and scanned the audience. "Do pray for me."

With a gauzy cap covering her hair, she wore the look of a cornered fox. And the bloodhounds were coming.

The knotted ends of string flipped about her thin shoulders as her dark eyes continued to search the crowd, from face to face.

Elizabeth nudged me. "It's as though she's looking for someone familiar."

I glanced at Elizabeth. "Wouldn't you?"

Elizabeth shrugged thoughtfully as we turned our attention back to the scaffold.

Lady Rochford's gaze darted along the front row. Chills shook my spine when her eyes met mine. She smiled broadly. A light seemed to turn on in her once-empty eyes, and she wrung her hands at her middle. Elizabeth's gasp was almost as loud as mine.

Lady Rochford arched her eyebrows and raised her voice. "Shall I say more?"

Is she asking me?

I shook my head gently and returned her smile. Mine wasn't as bright.

The chills that had shaken my spine coursed over my flesh and turned my blood to ice as Lady Rochford dropped to her knees. Still, she held my stare. Perhaps it was her familiar smile that bothered me most. Tears sprang to my eyes.

"She's gone mad," Elizabeth confirmed in my ear. "I believe it. I do, truly."

Jane's head sank onto the stained block. Hues of dark magenta, left by those unfortunates who met their eternity upon that very block, colored the wood. Lady Rochford adjusted herself, fidgeting about like a child, until her eyes found mine. Her mouth spread into a wide grin, once again bringing with it icy fingers of fear that tickled my throat.

The headsman, cloaked in a dirt brown cape, stepped forward. A gleaming double-edged axe lay against his shoulder. From behind a hooded leather mask, his icy gaze followed that of the condemned until it met mine.

"It's him," I managed through clenched teeth. My palms dampened once again.

Elizabeth's voice was a whisper. "Hey, is that not the man who spoke to you a moment ago?"

My hand found hers, and I gave it a squeeze.

Something in his eyes, blue as the June sky, made me flush. He paused a moment and gazed down at me from the scaffold before remembering his duty to the ladies of the hour.

He knelt next to Lady Rochford and began to speak. His voice rolled out over the silent crowd like a distant thunder. "Forgive me, m'lady."

"Of course, m'lord. I forgive you." Lady Rochford looked past him and offered me a small, girlish wave.

The executioner stood and moved behind her. Raising his axe

without further fanfare, he brought it down upon the naked neck of Lady Rochford with a whistling crack.

A raucous cheer went up from the crowd, but not from me. Ladies dressed in royal garb pushed past Elizabeth and me. One of them held a basket. When they picked up Lady Rochford's bloodied head, I saw her face. The foreboding grin was there, as wide as it had been in life, but the eerie light in her eyes was forever extinguished. A chilled tremble began in my fingers and traveled up until it reached my face.

Can the crowd see me shaking?

Behind the bloodied block, the fat man in purple removed Catherine Howard's velvet cloak. She looked so small, standing there in the same kind of shroud-like gown as Lady Rochford. Not at all like a queen, much less the Queen of England. I suppose she never really had been queen of anything, and now the whole of England—her included—knew Catherine Howard had never been anything more than a mere plaything to a king.

She inched toward the block, which was now covered in syrupy scarlet.

Did she step out of a yellow puddle of her own making?

I pushed myself onto the tips of my toes, but someone pushed in front of me and cut off my view.

Elizabeth's voice was a whisper. "It is rumored that she called for the block to be brought to her in the Tower last night. So she could practice laying herself upon it in a way not to cause embarrassment today." She nudged me. "In her practicing, do you think she accounted for the pool of blood?"

I ignored my cousin.

The same man who led both she and Lady Rochford through the crowd took Catherine's arm and helped her to the block. Her face was ghostly pale, and her legs trembled. Her voice trilled out as she began her speech. "My punishment is worthy and just as I stand here before God and all of you good Christian people. I beseech your mercy and prayers for my family and for my soul which will shortly arrive in Purgatory."

Purgatory? My brows knotted above my eyes. *Was Catherine a Catholic, like her family? Like me?*

"I die before you today a Queen," she said. Catherine paused, commanding the attention of all who stood before her. "But truly I tell you now, I would rather have died the wife of Thomas Culpeper."

A resounding gasp rose up from those in attendance.

"Her alleged lover who was executed for their passionate and lengthy affair!" Elizabeth's words strangled in her throat. "He was His Majesty's groom, and his head sits on London Bridge this very moment!"

Amid the low chatters that threatened to erupt into cacophony, Catherine knelt at the block and offered her forgiveness to the iron-eyed executioner. This time, he didn't glance at me. Something inside me wished he would.

I shook off the thought. *How absurd, Bridget. To earn the admiration of a murderer? Could one love a man who kills for a living?*

Catherine raised her face to the sky. A flock of geese honked as they flew over the castle, taking my misplaced thoughts of the executioner with them.

Only those of us on the first few rows heard Catherine's final words. "Life is so very beautiful."

Silence covered everyone in attendance like a shroud as the Queen of England lowered her head onto the block. I squeezed my eyes shut as the executioner drew back his blade, and the sickening thump that followed made me jump.

"Come ladies." The courtier with the white plume in his hat stepped in front of us. Behind him, Catherine's lifeless body oozed blood onto the straw. I tried not to look for her head. Luckily, I didn't see it when I pushed up onto my tiptoes.

"Ladies?"

I lowered myself back down slowly as several men dragged the headless corpse of the child queen from the scaffold.

"Ladies!" The courtier clapped. "Come now," he chirped, his face and voice much too bright given the occasion. "Let us prepare for the noon meal. You all must change in your given chambers, then appear in the dining hall in one hour's time." He waved his hands as though ushering cattle to slaughter. "Come come ladies! Much to be done!"

I felt eyes on me, burning, as I let myself be pushed along with the retreating crowd. Careful to keep a tight grip on Elizabeth's hand, I dared a glance over my shoulder. There on the scaffold stood the masked executioner, the deadly double-headed axe at his side. Scarlet liquid coated the edge and dripped from the sharp tip. Drop after drop fell dramatically into the straw below.

I was powerless to break away from his piercing stare and could only return it. His haunting image burned into my mind like a portrait. My stomach turned up in knots as the space between us widened. *What is so captivating about this ruthless, hooded headsman?*

KING HENRY VIII's CASTLE
His Majesty's Royal Dining Hall

I touched the embroidered napkin to the side of my mouth. Every fiber of my being wanted to spit the bite of roasted peacock into it, but I couldn't. Though His Majesty wasn't dining with us, I knew he was near.

Watching.

Calculating.

Judging.

As I glanced about, the gilded beak of the shiny blue bird in the center of the table caught my eye once again. Beyond it, Elizabeth laughed her musical laugh with the twins, a pair of tow-headed girls brought in from Dorset. Everything about those twins reminded me of summertime on the coast.

"Do you suppose it is real gold?" The wide-eyed girl from Surrey leaned closer to me. The edge of her scalloped collar dipped into her soup bowl. Her pinched mouth sat slightly off center of her thin chin. "On the beak, I mean."

With my back impossibly straight, I forced an awkward smile and offered her a small nod. My eyes watered as I let the bite of gamey bird slide down my throat. A hint of turkey haunted my palate as I felt for my cup of wine. All the while, I took care to keep the smile pasted on, on pain of vomiting up the royal dinner.

"I suppose it is," I managed to the girl from Surrey after I'd drained the last of my wine. "Here, take my napkin. For your lapel."

She accepted it. Her neck and cheeks flushed to rose red. "Oh! Thank you, really."

From nowhere, a servant appeared and refilled my mug. English wine rose to the brim, fuller and deeper scarlet than before.

I brushed a cocoa brown tendril of hair over my shoulder. "Thank you, sir."

He leaned close to my ear. "Compliments of the *King*."

My heart slapped the inside of my chest and my breath came faster. *Perhaps he is sending drinks around to all the girls.*

Careful not to call too much attention to myself, I turned slightly. The redheaded girl from Surrey still mopped at her front and her large, gray eyes watered just a bit. Sure enough, her mug was dry.

Elizabeth, lost in conversation with one of the twins from Dorset, picked up her mug. Her familiar voice rang out across the table like a beacon in my ears. "Do you suppose His Majesty would think me impolite if I were to ask for a refill?" Obviously already feeling the effects of the first helping, Elizabeth sniggered. "That wine is the best to have ever passed my lips!"

King Henry is watching.

My heartbeat, loud before, quickened to a pulsing gallop in my ears. The world spun around me and melted the dining hall into a fresco of colors, faces, and gold-beaked peacocks, still wearing their iridescent feathers. I squeezed shut my eyes and gripped the side of my chair. *Mother Mary, please intercede before I become ill.*

Someone clapped sharp and quick and sent a hush of quiet over my giggling tablemates. The courtier with the plume strode into the dining hall. His shoes, shiny black, clipped like horse hooves on a cobblestone street.

"Ladies." He bowed a deep bow. "Once again, it is so good of you all to have accepted the King's invitation and come to Court."

I nodded as the fictitious and all-too-familiar speech of thanks rolled off his tongue. Again. In my mind, I mouthed the words along with him. The man never strayed from a syllable.

You are the most desirable women in the whole of England. We are humbled to have shared the company of women such as yourselves.

His plump lips smacked together as he spoke, like two pigs wallowing in the mud and bumping their rears together. "You are the most desirable women in the whole of England."

A few women fanned themselves proudly.

"We are humbled to have shared the company of women such as yourselves."

Next, he will say, 'The King is greatly appreciative and eternally grateful'.

"The King is greatly appreciative and eternally grateful."

In all his puffed out, done up splendor, the courtier hiccupped and let his drunken stare meet all of ours.

Perhaps that is why nobody else's mugs were refilled.

When the large room was absolutely silent and every ounce of attention was centered on him, he spoke. "His Majesty, Henry the Eighth, King of England, Ireland, and France, thanks you all."

One of the Dorset twins began to clap a slow clap. Soon everyone had joined in, everyone except me. I made a show of moving my hands from beneath the table, tapping the top of my left with the fingers on my right.

Perhaps His Majesty will believe I was clapping all the while.

A veil of cold sweat cloaked my forehead.

The courtier held out his hands, successfully shushing the impromptu applause. "In accompaniment to his humble thanks, His Majesty also sends news." He broke from his standard soliloquy. "Her Majesty, the future Queen of England, sits among you!"

Another round of raucous applause and gasps filled the thick air. I hid a hiccup behind a pasted-on grin. The peacock centerpiece that stared at me from lifeless eyes seemed intent on haunting me.

The courtier grinned. His rotund cheeks were as shiny red as cherries. "His Majesty also sends a message of goodwill. He beseeches all of you to roam about the royal grounds at your leisure and rest well. While he must attend to business outside the castle this afternoon, he assures you all that word will come down tomorrow, answering the question of whom Her Majesty in fact is, in the manner of a formal announcement at breakfast."

Mother Mary, do not leave me. Please, in your Holy Son's Precious Name.

"For those of you charming elements of femininity who will *not* sit upon our country's throne, His Majesty will gladly write letters of recommendation on your behalf. Your King will ensure that you each gain a husband worthy of your royal stature and ladylike demeanor." The courtier bowed as low as his paunchy belly would allow. "And my dear ladies, do remember. For one of you today, you shall be roaming about what is *already* yours."

He turned sharply on his heel and disappeared, past a tapestry, and out the partially open door into the dark corridors of the castle.

All the girls turned to each other in a cloud of excited, giggling whispers. Even the redhead next to me turned, grinning, to the silent girl from Nottinghamshire whose pale face hadn't changed expression beneath her glistening raven locks since the morning—until now. All were giddy, enthusiastic.

All except me.

From behind the tapestry that hung almost to the floor, I caught sight of a slight movement. I adjusted in my seat and squinted into the shadows.

The tapestry moved again. This time, it was pushed out from the wall, as if by an arm. A gleam of light from a slatted window glinted off a golden necklace. My breath caught in my throat. An unblinking eye stared back at me.

That be him. King Henry VIII.

A rash of tremors shinnied down my spine. I covered my mouth with one hand as the other girls began to rise from their plush seats. However, staring into the brown eye of my Sovereign Lord, I sat paralyzed in mine.

Before I could rise from my stupor, before I could dip into a curtsey, the brown eye and glinting golden necklace disappeared. I rubbed my eyes.

Did that really happen? Perhaps I was dreaming. Perhaps it was the wine—

The sound of the heavy brown door sliding across the stone floor met my ears.

I wasn't dreaming.

The tapestry hung still. Quickly as I had spotted him, Henry vanished.

Footfalls, slightly out of step, grew softer as the girls about me chattered on, oblivious to all that just happened.

I rose. The chills icing my body dulled to a warm sweat. Something in my stomach, probably the peacock, threatened to revolt.

Since we were released until morning, I dodged the bright glances from my fellow Ladies-of-Choice and started toward the same door that Henry and the Courtier had used.

Elizabeth spoke loudly to the girls who still circled the table. "Let us make a pact. Whichever of us becomes Queen, she shall appoint the rest of us as her Ladies-in-Waiting."

Squeals answered her and echoed in the dining hall.

Unable to help myself, I peeked into the dark shadows behind the tapestry. Of course, it concealed no one. At least not anymore. I pushed the heavy wooden door until it slid outward in the same wood-scraping-stone sound I'd heard moments before.

Elizabeth's musical voice tinkled along the stones behind me, just as it had when we were children together back home at Throckmorton Priory. "That way, we are all ensured a place a Court and not one of us must return home a failure."

I shook my head as the door closed behind me.

Elizabeth, really. Appoint these women as your Ladies-in-Waiting? Women who want your place on the throne?

I shook my head again and whispered to myself as I picked my way down the halls in a feeble attempt to locate my chambers.

You aren't even seated upon the throne of England, yet already you make grave mistakes.

The stone hall ended abruptly, the passageway was obviously sealed off some time ago. I turned and started back the way I'd come and let my fingers trace the wall for comfort. Still, I mentally flogged my cousin.

If every woman around you wants your job, chances are she will stop at nothing until she gets it.

I turned another corner, acutely aware that the servants who had been bustling about were no more.

If worrying over the wrath of your husband isn't bad enough, you would have your ladies to fear as well. One may poison you... or arrange an accident... or sleep with the King and ask him to arrange your murder...

The candelabra above me flickered and sent a shiver coursing over my skin. Lady Rochford's eerie, familiar smile flashed in my mind.

Stop it Bridget. You're simply lost and it has been a trying day. I sucked in a deep breath. *Now, try to remember—*

A hand fell, feather light, upon my shoulder. "Lady Bridget."

I didn't have to turn around to know who shared this space with me. The hiss in his aged voice brought a churn to my stomach, the same brand of churning that had almost overtaken me when I spied his brown eye peering out from behind the tapestry.

Still facing the wall, I dipped into a stiff curtsey. "Your Majesty," I croaked.

Where had he come from?

His hand flitted away from my shoulder like a bird from a dead bough. "Turn around, let me look at you."

I chewed my lip and did as I was told.

Despite being dressed in the finest robes and threads, and despite the noble, jewel-encrusted crown upon his head, the man before me was inexplicably old. Bags beneath his eyes held all the weight of the worries of yesteryear. Thick wrinkles had taken the place of what was probably once taut, tanned skin. Once upon a time, he was probably a sight to behold. But now?

Tales of his robust, brawny good looks filled the English countryside when I was a girl, however those years were spent on women who weren't me. Had I grown old with this man, I would have seen the beauty in the wrinkles since I would have shared in the making of memories and the laughter that outlasted them. Try as I might, I couldn't see the handsome young man hidden inside this broken shell of a murderous old blaggard.

A gangrenous odor, understated yet still present, wafted up from his bad leg, just as tales suggested. The stench brought a sting to my eyes and a burn to my nose.

His glistening brown eyes searched me, taking no care to be subtle or even hint at romance. Finally, his gaze met mine. I tried not to show disgust as I returned his stare, though his was ravenous with a hunger that I would never reciprocate.

"Thank you for the wine at dinner, Your Majesty."

"You are a marvelous creature, Lady Bridget," he breathed, ignoring my gratitude. "Hair the color of baked bread." He fingered a tendril before continuing. "Eyes like burning embers, jade or emeralds." Ever slow, he let his fingers trail from my hair down my cheek. "Skin as innocent and pure as milk and honey..."

Though his hand cupped my cheek, Henry's lust-laden eyes fell to my chest before continuing down my tight blue bodice. "This dress becomes you. It is no doubt filled with other delicious treasures just waiting to be discovered." His hoarse voice fell to a whisper. "And *conquered.*"

Revulsion rose and fell in my stomach. Lady Rochford's haunted smile. The Queen's wetting herself before a crowd of people who hated her. Their untimely deaths. These fresh memories, punctuated by the sickening thunks of rolling heads, were all too raw. And this man and his royal whims had caused it all.

The burning blue eyes of the headsman came to mind from nowhere; the way he'd stared at me as I left the Tower Green. The way I'd stared back for no reason I could properly place.

Henry reached down and adjusted himself. "Perhaps we can journey to uncharted lands right now." In an instant, I was pressed against the wall, and his exposed member, stiff with want, pressed against my thigh as he struggled with the layers of my dress.

Emotion tightened my throat. I pushed back against his shoulders, but bit my tongue. Any wrong word would cost me my head.

Is my maidenhead such a price to pay for my life?

"Ah," he groaned, successfully exposing my lower half. "Do tell me you consent, beautiful Bridget."

Before I could answer, a torch lit the far end of the hall. "The horses are saddled and ready, Your Majesty."

Henry's lusty want went flaccid. "I'm coming," he answered. His voice echoed off the ancient stones with an almost divine authority. I shifted my hips and sent the layers of my dress cascading back where they were supposed to be. Down.

Henry stepped back, his eyes on me. He took no qualms to be modest as he tucked himself back into his folds of clothing. When he was tucked securely away, he spread his arms wide. "M'lady." His head dipped slightly from years of practice. "The next time we meet, I pray you conceive my son. Until then, I bid you good day."

With that he turned and strode, slightly out of step, to the torchman waiting at the end of the hall. As he rounded the corner out of sight, I realized my hands were not trembling. They were not shaking nor were they shuddering. They were *quaking* with violent tremors, despite the thick and humid warmth of the castle air.

The English night fell soft and velvet black about the royal grounds. Stars, bright and silver, twinkled like jewels above us as Elizabeth broke the easy quiet. "Who do you suppose it is?"

"Hmm?" I stepped off the path that led back to the castle from the garden. I still hadn't fully recovered from my brief, unsuccessful encounter with the King, despite a long night-time walk in the garden with Elizabeth. "What now?"

"Which girl do you suppose is Queen?"

The drawbridge was still down, despite the late hour. Word had come back that His Majesty's manly urges were renewed at the prospect of a new queen and the business that pulled him from the castle had indeed been nothing more than a hunting trip. It was also said that he swore *not* to return to the castle until he'd shed the lifeblood of the largest wild boar in the Royal Forest, with which to honor this new queen.

Manly urges.

Elizabeth and I walked toward the downed drawbridge. "I figure it be you, Cousin," I lied.

Something tied my tongue, and the instinct of sheer self-preservation warned me to eke not a word to anyone of my near-dalliance with the King. "He no doubt heard your musical laugh and knew at once he must take you to wife."

Elizabeth flushed, her cheeks matching the hue of her scarlet and gold dress. "I figured more on you." Her voice was quiet. "After all, you are a rare beauty Bridget. And would make a stately Queen of England." She glanced at me, the light in her eyes flickering back to a flame. "And Catholic, too."

I knew how much those words must scald her tongue. Elizabeth and I were nothing if not competitive while growing up, not to mention on different sides of the Reformation. She never took defeat well.

Still, something in her face told me she had made peace with this, of all things. She took my hand. "Tell me you will appoint me as your head Lady-in-Waiting."

A whiff of jasmine thickened the air around us. "Your figuring is wrong, Cousin." I untwisted my hand from hers and let the cool quiet envelope us again. A moment later, we came upon a sitting place.

I sunk down upon the obscure stone bench, bathed in moonlight. It looked to have been in that same spot since William the Conqueror's time, the trunk of the tree having grown into the bench itself. I leaned against it, taking no qualms to be careful with the blue silk gown. *Edged in purple.* "Tell me, do you remember how the straw soaked up Catherine's blood this morning?"

Elizabeth eyed me, slowly taking the chilled seat beside me. "Yes actually. I do."

I looked around and appreciated the exquisite hedgerows and rosebushes. "I remember the fear, Elizabeth. The fear in her eyes, the puddle at her feet of her own making." I swallowed back the emotion I thought I kept in check.

Elizabeth patted my shoulder, but the tears that pricked my eyes still came. "And poor Lady Rochford. Why was she looking at me that way?"

"There there now." My cousin wrapped her arms around me and danced around my question. "Their transgressions are simply avoidable for the next queen."

I sniffled and pulled away. "Are they Elizabeth? Really?"

She followed my train of thought. "Bridget, come now. Those women brought their punishments upon themselves. They said so from their own lips. This is the title of *Queen of England* that hangs in the balance. I have a sneaking suspicion you have it; you just don't know it yet."

You have no idea just how much I know.

I pushed up from the cold bench and swiped at my eyes with the back of my hand. A few threads snapped, unwilling to be released from the ancient bark. "No Cousin. You're wrong." I glanced over my shoulder.

Now I am the hare. And the bloodhounds are coming.

The drawbridge led into the Royal Forest. "No matter who was chosen today as the next Queen of England—" I looked back at my cousin, sitting on the stone bench, eyes wide and fearful. "It shall *not* be me."

"Bridget!" Elizabeth's scolding voice sounded much like Aunt Lady Denny's. Of course, she who was left to care for me was much too interested in her own popularity at Court to be bothered with the likes of her daughter or her orphaned niece, no matter how much they needed her.

I lifted my skirts and turned toward the drawbridge. Without bothering to say goodbye, I dashed toward my only chance at freedom.

"Bridget, *stop!*"

I didn't stop until I reached the downed drawbridge. I glanced through the opening and spotted the guard. He'd placed his back in a corner so as to give the illusion of attentiveness. I stared for a moment. Watching. Praying. Sure enough, his head nodded a few times and then dipped low to his chest.

Elizabeth's voice was a hiss along the night breezes. "Bridget! You'll be killed for this. As will I!"

These woods surrounding the castle are deep and dark. Surely they hold many secrets. Perhaps there is room for one more. Without looking back or thinking too incredibly far into the future, I slipped into the dark cover of the royal forest.

THE KING'S FOREST

Branches tore at my hair and dress as I ran. My chest heaved against the impossible whale-bone corset. *His Majesty and all his men are out in these very woods. Should they find me—*

The swift chop of the headsman's axe echoed in my skull. I kicked out of my azure slippers and ran faster beneath the deep canopy.

Sounds of the night creatures amplified as I struggled to catch my breath. Images of Henry and his gleaming brown eye, peering at me from behind every tree trunk, faded until he became a wild boar, largest in the whole of England, running for his life, crashing through the understory.

Tears streamed down my cheeks and I leaned against the trunk of an ivy-encased trunk. The darkness was almost tangible, and I was certain that brown eye was out there. Staring at me from the deep black. Watching. Waiting. Lusting.

Somewhere nearby, a dog barked.

His Majesty has discovered my absence and set the dogs after me.

I pushed off like a sprinter and dashed blindly through the wilds. I didn't care where I wound up, just so long as it was nowhere near Henry or the castle. My jagged breath clawed at my throat as I refused to give in to the sharp pains that stabbed my sides, or the misbegotten roots and rocks that jabbed at my stockinged feet.

Finally, I slowed as I entered a clearing, illuminated by the moonlight, through the sudden parting of leaves.

Is that a light?

I rubbed my bleary eyes and willed my breathing to slow. My heart thundered in my ears as the tiny stone cottage, built into side of a small knoll, came into focus before me. Just as I thought, a lone candle lit the front window.

In the distance, it came again. Sharp. Like a slap to a cold cheek. Another dog bark.

I chewed my lower lip and rushed the door. My quivering fingers rapped the ancient wood in staccato succession. And waited.

Nothing.

I knocked again, louder this time, and pressed my ear to the wooden slats.

The door creaked inward.

Without bothering with a second time-consuming thought, I stepped inside. My heartbeat pulsed in my ears as I pushed the heavy door shut behind me. I leaned against it, eyes closed. In this moment, I was safe. Safe from the wild boar. Safe from the bloodhounds. Safe from the peeping brown eye.

At least for now.

I opened my eyes and dared a peek around my new surroundings. A roughhewn chair sat before a crooked hearth, and a candle flickered in the only window. Across the way, a door set partially open to what was probably somebody's sleeping quarters. A black kettle hung in the fireplace that had long grown cold. Above the mantle hung a gleaming, familiar object. "Surely not."

I rubbed my eyes.

"Surely not," I whispered again. As much as I wished they had, my eyes had not deceived me. A double headed axe hung above the fireplace.

My breath caught in my throat as I stepped to the middle of the quaint cottage, not wanting to remember where I'd seen that axe before. I turned slowly and prayed for any sign of the cottage's owner. Perhaps a simple parkkeeper and his wife. Anyone, so as long as the owner wasn't—

Then, there it was. On the middle roof timber. The tell-tale brown hooded mask, hanging innocently enough.

Blood drained from my face, and my knees began to shake. I smoothed wildly at my hair and chewed my lip. "I've gone from the coliseum stadium into the lion's den."

The scraping of the door along the dirt floor made me jump. Before I could find a place to hide, a shirtless man wearing only britches stepped inside. Droplets of water dotted his chest and hung like diamonds from his damp, black locks. Freshly scrubbed, his muscular arms shone in the glow of candlelight as he rubbed his glistening hair with a cloth.

I swallowed hard as the shirtless man froze in the doorway and his ice blue eyes met mine. Again.

I recognized him at once, even without his brown hooded mask. With all the luck of a condemned man who escaped the gallows only to find himself in the torture chamber, I'd found my way into the quarters of His Majesty's private executioner.

My fingers searched the stone wall behind me.

Perhaps I can make it out the door, if I can just get by him—

Catching myself staring at his smooth, chiseled chest, I turned my face away.

Why had you not expected such a handsome creature to belong to those eyes, those striking blue eyes.

Words as gruff as I remembered filled the cottage. "How did you find me?" His eyes narrowed to fiery slits. "Why are you here?"

My tongue untied as I began in shaky words. "Have—have you been sent to kill me?" I gulped. "Sir?"

"Sir?" The executioner arched a dark eyebrow. "Perhaps we should exchange pleasantries before talk of killing. Don't you agree?" He stepped inside and pushed the door shut, effectively sealing my exit. "I'm Jean St. Bromaine. Seems you've found your way into my home."

Fear chopped the politeness from my words as I tried to place his accent. *A mixture of French and Welsh perhaps?* "I know who you are. I saw you this morning."

"Ah, yes. I knew I recognized you. But the question remains, who are *you*?"

I dug my fingers into the rock wall behind me. A hot flush crept up my neck. "Forgive me. I am Lady Bridget. I was brought to court—"

My thought trailed off as I realized Jean was no longer listening. He turned his back to me as he continued to dry his hair with the cloth. Muscles rippled beneath his skin, giving rise to an odd emotion in my stomach. We stood together in awkward silence.

Finally, he flung the damp cloth over a peg beside the door and turned back to face me. "Good evening, *Lady* Bridget."

My eyes widened at his unspoken insult. My tongue grew bold, and I let go of the stone wall. "Tell me, Jean, why are your quarters not in the castle? Or more appropriately, the Tower?"

I tilted my chin as I had seen Lady Denny do, and elicited a smoldering look from Jean.

He removed a white cloth shirt from over the back of the chair and drew it over his head and arms. Pulling it down, he covered his chiseled chest and stomach before he spoke. "I do my job well. In return, the King affords me the simple luxury of choosing my own quarters."

I glanced at the headsman's axe that hung above the mantle, almost a living thing itself. The same curved, double sided blade that took the lives of Catherine Howard and Lady Rochford just this morning no longer dripped with syrupy blood, but instead gleamed.

He followed my gaze. A smile raised the corners of his full lips. "And as you see, I choose to live as far from the *castle* and as far away from the goings on at Court as possible." He sunk into the lone chair, a look of contentment on his darkly shadowed face. "After all, I usually see the faces that fill the His Majesty's Court in my own time."

I stared at him, any words I could say refusing to untangle themselves and escape my tongue.

Jean linked his fingers together across his chest. "What I mean to say is that those who are favorites at Court one day, often wind up trembling upon my chopping block the next."

"Yes," I mused. "I can see how that would be true. That is precisely the reason I'm here, as well." Muscles in my neck I hadn't realized were tense began to twitch and relax.

Jean sat forward, his elbows on his knees. "How about a pot of tea?" His gauzy shirt drooped a bit at the neckline. I tried not to let my gaze fall to what the shirt kept hidden. The curious blush that appeared with Jean still burned in my cheeks.

"Tea? Yes, please." I nodded. "Thank you."

Bridget, what has come over you?

He rose easily, like water rippling over the rocks in a stream, and gestured wide with his arm. "Do take the chair."

I took my full skirt in my hands, stepped to where Jean motioned, and did exactly as he commanded. As he moved about the cottage, I was powerless not to track his every move. The seat was still warm. I sucked in a breath and willed my beating heart to slow.

The fire crackled merrily as Jean fed it branch after branch. Taking a silver pot from a peg, he squatted and filled it with water dipped from the bucket on the floor. "The water's fresh, Lady Bridget. I drew it just before I bathed in the river."

"Please, just Bridget." Something in Jean's words about distancing himself from Court had a kernel of truth in it for me, too.

"As you wish, Bridget. Now tell me. Why are you here? In the middle of the night? In my home." He thrust the full kettle alongside the fire. A bit of water sloshed over the side and sizzled in the flames. "*Alone.*"

My aunt's words scolded sharply from somewhere. *Don't fidget Bridget!* Sure enough, I was twirling and rubbing the purple ends of my dress.

Remembering myself, I clasped my hands together at my middle just as she'd taught me. "My cousin Elizabeth and I were visited by two royal courtiers. They chose us to come to Court and be among the ladies His Majesty would choose from for his next wife."

Jean rose and took a pair of small tin cups from the mantle. "And in His Majesty's wisdom, he made sure all potential Queens filled the front row of the latest Queen's execution." His musical voice was a growl in his throat. "I knew I never had seen all of those beautiful faces before."

From a small box, he plucked out a pinch of black tea leaves. He rolled each pinch between his fingers, crushing them and letting them fall to the bottom of each cup. Something twisted in my stomach as I watched his practiced fingers demolish the tea leaves. I swallowed hard and crossed my ankles.

His skin was softer than anything I'd touched before when our fingers met this morning—

"Bridget?"

I jumped. "Yes? I'm sorry, I was just—"

Daydreaming of your soft skin touching mine, in places nobody has touched before.

I studied my lap, embarrassed, and completely at a loss as to what to say.

"I asked if you thought it odd that the front row of Catherine's execution was filled with potential mates."

This man is a murderer, Bridget. He has killed more people for profit than... than...

"I did find it odd." Still, I couldn't look at him. "Do you suppose he had a reason for wanting us to witness the executions?" Something flashed in my mind. Something about the way that brown eye had watched me from behind the tapestry. My modest shyness retreated to the shadowed corners of the cottage. "It was a warning, wasn't it?"

Jean filled both cups with boiling water and handed one to me. I took it with weak hands. "No, not a warning, m'lady. Coming from King Henry, that was a promise."

My bones seemed to turn to jelly beneath my skin. "That's why I'm so dreadfully afraid. That's why, after all the unwanted attentions at the noon meal, I knew I must escape."

Jean perched himself on the hand-hewn table, just inches from me. "Unwanted attentions?"

I nodded, the flush in my cheeks having cooled to an eerie pale. "My cup of wine ran empty. A groomsman refilled it and whispered, *Compliments of the King*." I stared into my cup as the water steeped the black leaves into what I hoped would be a strong tea. "Nobody else's cup was refilled."

Somewhere nearby a cricket began to sing, setting my tale of woe to music. "Then, one of the courtiers who came to my house marched in and said that His Majesty had chosen a queen and she was indeed among us, seated at the table. When I saw a brown eye peeking at me, leering really, from behind a tapestry, I knew it was His Majesty." A tremble started in my fingers and overtook my hands. Tea sloshed onto my lap.

Jean took my cup, gently set it on the floor with his before covering both my fidgeting hands with his. They were so much softer than I remembered. "So you ran away then."

Moisture welled in my eyes. In this moment, I wasn't sitting helplessly in the home of His Majesty's executioner. I was transported to the solemn quiet safety of a Catholic confessional. I drew in a breath.

"I fear it's me. I fear His Majesty has chosen me for his next Queen. And I couldn't stay. They promised to make the formal announcement in the morning." A lone drop escaped my eye and slid down my lashes, dangling only a moment before falling onto Jean's hand. I sniffled.

"I know the fear you speak of." His thumb stroked my hands. "Which is why I must do my job well. To end that very fear. Quickly. Without pain."

Emotion caught in my throat, and I raised my face. Jean, still stroking my hands, stared back at me with eyes like blue flames. "Thank you for taking away that bloody tremble from my hands."

A small smile lifted his lips and chased away the ghosts of those whose lives were ended too soon. His voice emerged quiet, breathy. "Bridget, have you ever loved?"

I flexed my fingers beneath his comforting grasp and let my touch dance along his palm. "No. I've not, though I suppose I would have been *loved* had I not escaped the King this afternoon."

"Come again?"

I shifted my weight on the seat. The bottom was tight leather lashed to the wooden frame, probably made by Jean himself. It was surprisingly comfortable. "I was lost, trying to find my way to my chambers, and found myself in a hallway with an abrupt end."

Jean nodded. "And lit with candles, no servants, and no doors. Am I right?"

My jaw went slack. "Yes. How did you—?"

"They're traps, rather effective. His Majesty likes to hunt, for anything. The thrill of the chase is what drives him on in his old age. Like a cat with a mouse. Once the mouse is caught—"

I followed Jean's pointed glance up to his axe. A sheen of sweat rolled over me like an ocean wave, leaving me feeling nearly weightless.

"Nor have I." Jean's voice changed the conversation back to the tone of a warm confessional. Safe. Private. Words spoken here only meant for one set of ears. "Nor have I loved, I mean."

For a moment, I was a fish out of water. My mouth calling for air that just wouldn't come. How close had I been to death today? Closer than I cared to be.

"I had a woman once. A Welsh maiden. She claimed to love me and to want to be married. Until she found out what I did for my life's work. Then she left."

Jean broke our grasp and plucked up our cups. "I suppose she loved with as much sincerity, or lack thereof, as His Majesty loves anything. Aside from self-pleasure." He drew a long sip off the top of his tea. "For with true love, you should never bear to part from it without the intent to return. Never. And certainly never execute it."

"I agree." I accepted my tea from Jean's hand and swirled it, then took a sip. Strong, but not overpowering. Just right. "All must make their way in this life. I certainly don't judge you by your station." My words, full to bursting with unspoken meaning, hung thick in the air about us.

Jean drained his cup. He leaned slightly and reached out with those long fingers.

A horrid thought grasped my mind and threatened to choke all the romantic feelings from between us.

This hand deals death like royal men deal cards. Yet it advances.

Jean's hand stopped short and brushed a lock of my hair with his thumb. Slowly, his soft fingers trailed from my forehead down my cheek. My eyes closed on their own and soaked up the sizzling trail they left in their wake. "And I admire you for having the courage to run away from certain death."

I couldn't respond. Everything inside me seemed to have turned to stone.

Jean brushed my lips with his thumb and sent my heart skipping like a flat rock across the water. My eyes sprang open and a different brand of tremble shook my fingers. I pushed myself up on wobbly knees. "Your cup is empty. Please, let me fill it."

Nervous flutters in my stomach made my movements jumpy and odd as I accepted his cup and stepped to the hearth.

Oh Bridget, really. Do you suppose it possible to honestly fall in love with a man over one spot of tea? And of all men, the man who murders at the King's whim? I heard my hoarse breath, coming quickly, so I fought to control it. *And do you suppose he is really capable of love. And could he possibly love me?*

The King's Forest
The Home of the Headsman

I replaced the kettle beside the fire and stood. "There now, here we go," I started. A warm hand from behind cupped my face and trailed down my neck. My words turned to almost forgotten thoughts. A gasp escaped my lips as Jean's long fingers circled about my throat.

His breath warmed my ear. Jean's other hand snaked about my waist, erasing the space between us. "Bridget," he breathed as though he were punctuating a prayer with my name.

I sucked in a shuddering breath, lost in the feel of his hands on my body. Exploring. Soothing. Perhaps a bit teasing. My eyes closed on their own as I looped my arm up and around the neck of the executioner who stole my heart. His long, ebony locks tickled my arm and turned my insides to mush.

I turned into his strong, waiting arms. Our lips met at once. Jean's mouth worked against mine, letting loose a lifetime of unspent passion.

Never having experienced anything of the sort, my pulse raced through my body like a great steed through the hunter's green. My lips parted against Jean's hungry kiss as his fingers traced my face before winding into my hair. Jean wrested his fingers deep into my hair and pulled my head back slowly until my throat was fully exposed to his ravenous passions.

His name wisped from my lips as my fingers dug into his muscled back. "Jean." Wanting ached within me, tightening unrealized muscles and sending a seductive pulse through my secret places. The thick, sweet scent of Jean's earthen home combined with his woodsy musk left my head spinning, as though we'd been drinking sweet brandy instead of black tea.

Damp, dark locks laced his strong jaw and curled down, tickling my throat. His lightly stubbled face scratched me as he guided my lips back to his with gentle hands. My quivering fingers cupped his face. Tracing and memorizing every curve. Every crevasse. I brushed a dark curl from the thick fringe of lashes that ringed those icy azure eyes that seemed to see straight through me, straight into my very soul.

"Bridget, be mine tonight." His high-boned cheeks colored and his voice fell to a near imperceptible level. "Tonight and every night thereafter. Always."

The whinny of a horse outside made us jump in unison. I kicked over both teacups. "Do you always have visitors this time of night?"

"No."

A sharp knock rapped on the door.

"Go, hide yourself in my bedchamber." Jean brushed my lips with a warm kiss, but all the love and light were gone from his eyes, puffed out, like a candle. "Do hurry."

I did as I was told. No sooner had I pushed the door shut to Jean's bedroom did I hear the familiar, heavy scrape across the floor. Terrified and cloaked in complete darkness, I felt blindly for the bed.

Jean's voice, thick with a feigned yawn, found my ears. "Good evening, Dudley. What brings you out of the dungeon at such a terrible hour?"

The dungeon?

My pounding heart stopped cold and took my breath with it. *Dear heavens, it is His Majesty's torturer.*

Grabbing up what I hoped was a sheet, I flung it about my shoulders and searched for a corner. A deep, dark corner.

"Did me ole ears deceive me, or did I hear a lady's voice? I hopes I'm not interruptin'." The silence that followed was deafening. "Tell me true Jean, did Rhiannon come back from the Welsh Marches?"

I imagined Dudley to be a short, hunched troll of a man with one large eye and a face covered in growths. He would be looking over his shoulder, eyes crazy, his snaggled teeth yellow in the moonlight.

"Yes, she did. Just tonight actually."

The torturer's voice bubbled out, excited. "What did ole Dudley tell you? I knowed she'd come back. Only took a few months to tie up her affairs in Wales, see?"

"It was a year."

"Never mind that. I won't keep you. I just come 'cause the King sent me here himself. To fetch you, I mean."

"Oh?"

In my mind's eye, I could see Jean cock an eyebrow and cross his arms.

"His Majesty has chosen a queen from the Ladies-of-Choice. Lady Bridget Denny."

Fear knotted my stomach and danced its chilled dance down my spine. I pressed a fist to my lips to keep from crying.

Jean's voice was steady. "That's wonderful news. But it doesn't answer the question as to why His Majesty sent you here."

Dudley's voice was a coarse whisper. "When he returned from his hunt, The King went to visit her bedchamber as a husband visits that of his wife, only to find it *empty*. This was a great displeasure to His Majesty."

"I imagine so."

"He learnt through other Ladies-of-Choice that Bridget wished *not* to be married to the King."

Jean feigned a gasp. "No."

"Aye, it be so. And in fact, disappeared under the cover of night from the very castle walls that were to be hers."

My pulse pounded in my head.

Elizabeth, my own flesh and blood, betrayed me.

"Men have been sent to find her. I was sent here, to recall you to the castle. For when she's brought in—" I heard his voice turn up in a grin.

Jean was silent, but must have made a discontented face.

The torturer stammered over his words. "The King was very put out. He will not stand to be humiliated. We are to have the girl brought in and handled appropriately by first light."

Terror shook my bones. Here under this very roof were the two most powerful, death-dealing men in the kingdom. The first, capable of doling out such pains and misery that one would wish for nothing but death. The second, capable of granting that wish with one striking blow. Two wolves on the hunt for blood. *My* blood.

Wrapped in a sheet and cloaked in dreadful darkness, I found myself, again, to be the lowly hare.

Jean's voice cut through the silence like a knife through warm bread. "I will report to the castle straight away. Tell me, will you be combing the King's Forest in search of this Bridget?"

"Yes, of course. The King's men have probably set the bloodhounds after her by now." He snorted. "I don't have to tell you that His Majesty has prepared a handsome reward for the man, or *men*, who brings her in. His Majesty also promises I will have time with her first, in the dungeon, before she comes to you. Unless of course, locking her in the Tower after torture be His Majesty's pleasure—"

Jean cut him off. "Perhaps we can split this handsome reward you speak of. I'll go south. You take the north trail. I'll meet you outside the castle gates just before sun up."

"Aye. We can do that. But ole Dudley has an advantage."

A pause echoed in the silence.

Jean spoke. "Does that blue slipper there belong to Lady Bridget?"

"It do. I done found the pair of them in the forest. I feel I'm close to her. Close to catching her. And when I do…"

The burn of tears lit my throat aflame, but this time, they didn't wet my eyes.

A moment later, the door scraped across the floor before clicking shut.

The axe gleamed in the firelight behind Jean as he opened the bedroom door. With no windows from which to escape, I ducked deeper into the darkest corner.

"Bridget?"

Fear closed my throat.

Jean's voice was a hiss in the black. "Bridget!"

Finally, a rogue tear slid down my cheek.

"Come out, Bridget."

I peeked out from my hiding place. I couldn't place the expression on Jean's face and wasn't sure I wanted to.

"Come Bridget." Jean extended his hand. "We must go."

THE ROYAL FOREST
A Secret Place

"Jean?"

"Shush," he grunted.

The arboreal canopy thickened, blotting out the silver twinkles against the black night, as Jean drew me down a forest path that only he could see. The understood rule was a roar in my ears: absolute and total *silence*. I measured my breathing and tried not to pant at the pace Jean set for us. It was as though wherever we were going, we were already late.

Uneasiness quaked beneath the chestfuls of heavy pine air and twisted and turned in my stomach like a surfeit of eels. The thought of breaking away from Jean's grasp tickled the back of my mind.

Does he mean to turn me in for His Majesty's handsome reward? This man who kills for money?

The world was sooty and seemed to be closing in.

Perhaps if I slip my hand from his, I can simply fade into the black—

Before I could put my plan into action, Jean slowed to a stop. "Right about here," he muttered. He reached out with a fist and banged on what I thought was a tree trunk. A pool of soft yellow candlelight warmed the darkness from a window I hadn't realized was there till now.

I slipped my hand from Jean's, but the thought of escape scurried away like shadows from the newborn light. As my eyes adjusted, I studied the rock building, perfectly nestled in this ancient grove of gnarled trees. I ran my hand down the worn cobblestones. "Why, this is a..." I turned to Jean. "A chapel?"

Jean's voice was a whisper, quiet as the breeze. "This is Father Gabriel's home. He moved from London into this old chapel when His Majesty began burning Catholics. I come here for confession after every execution. And sometimes in between."

My racing mind struggled to keep up with his words.

"You're... Catholic?"

Jean took my hands in his. "Marry me, Bridget. Be mine. Always. For I was yours the moment I held your handkerchief this very morning."

A splintery wooden door creaked open, and the space was filled at once by a small man. His face was weathered and wrinkled, and a smile crinkled the corners of his eyes. "Ah, Jean St. Bromaine. Welcome again, my son."

The old man extended his knotted hands in greeting, his fingers as gnarled as the very trees that enveloped his chapel.

"Evening Father. Forgive us for coming so late." Jean knelt on one knee before Father Gabriel. "This is Lady Bridget. She was chosen as His Majesty's next queen."

"I see. So why is she not at Court?" Something in Father Gabriel's round face told me he already knew.

Jean kept his head bent low. "Lady Bridget believes that her appointment as the wife of His Majesty is but a slow and inevitable sentence of certain death. I feel she is correct in her observation."

"As do the good people of England," Father Gabriel agreed. Letting go of Jean's hand, he turned and extended one to me. "My child."

Taking it, I dipped to one knee. "Father Gabriel."

Jean continued. "Father, I wish to take Lady Bridget as my true

and only wife. Now. This night. If she shall choose to have me."
He peeked back at me.

Realizing my ignorance in doubting his intentions, my lower
lip began to tremble. Here he was, putting his life in perhaps even
graver danger than my own. For when the King's men discovered
Jean missing, not to mention having taken me to wife, I knew
in my heart that, should we be captured, Jean's relationship with
Dudley would take on a wholly new level of meaning in the dank
recesses of the royal dungeon.

"I will never doubt you again," I whispered. "Not now, and not
when you become my true husband tonight."

Once again moisture welled in my eyes and sent my world
a-shimmer. The strange emotion that appeared whenever Jean was
near had a name. I knew it now. That name was *love*.

Jean's strong-jawed face broke into soft planes of pride and
pleasure. From behind my veil of watery emotion, it appeared
that a tear tracked down Jean's cheek as well.

Jean sniffed and drew the back of his hand across his eyes.
"Father, they have already turned out the bloodhounds. And placed
a handsome reward on Lady Bridget's head."

Father Gabriel helped me to my feet. "Then we ought to begin.
Jean, extinguish the candle." Turning in his flowing white robe,
Father Gabriel disappeared into the tiny chapel. I followed as Jean's
hand trembled on the small of my back. Once inside, he pulled
the door shut and snuffed out the candle.

Down a narrow staircase lined with a knotted tree branch ban-
ister, I had to feel my way through the thick blackness. Jean's hand
resumed its place on my back and gave me courage in the darkness.
Still, my heart refused to slow.

A door creaked below, and soft candlelight flooded into the dank
stairway. Father Gabriel disappeared into the quaint sanctuary
that opened up before us. I hurried down the remaining steps and
gasped at what lay before us.

Father Gabriel took his place behind a stone altar, a small silver cross before him. Our Lord and Savior was affixed there by our mortal sins. Candles glittered along the walls, highlighting small statues of the Holy Family. I did the sign of the cross before taking my knees in front of the altar.

In nominae Patris et Filii et Spiritus Sancti.

Jean lowered himself beside me, his head bowed in our shared reverence.

Father Gabriel did the sign of the cross over us and began the ancient Latin recitation that had joined souls together for centuries. Something broken and terrified within my spirit renewed with Father Gabriel's healing words and soothing voice as the ceremony carried on. Peace, solid and strong in the knowledge of my future with Jean, be it for hours or decades, filled my skipping heart.

The thought of His Majesty's absolute fury upon finding out what I'd done, with his executioner to boot, tried to niggle in during Father Gabriel's final prayers.

The Iron Maiden. The Scavenger's Daughter. The Pear. Tales of people locked in coffin-like cages with hungry rats and left to be eaten alive.

I shook my head. Madness could take its toll wondering what bone-breaking practices were being planned for you. Hellish tortures were exacted day and night in His Majesty's dungeon at the practiced hands of Dudley and, should the King's men capture us, the most nightmarish would be reserved for me—and Jean. We would be left begging for the merciful stroke of the headsman's axe that would no doubt be late in coming, if ever it should.

"Bless you both." Father Gabriel's voice flowed like calm waters through a rushing river. "Wherever your journey takes you, go with God."

Standing in the partially concealed doorway of the illicit chapel, I clutched Jean's hand as though my very life depended on it.

Jean kept his voice low. "Thank you, Father. Our final destination is France. Calais."

I listened attentively.

Jean had a plan of escape for us all along.

"But first we must reach the coast, then find a ferryman willing to smuggle us the 26 miles across the Strait of Dover."

Before the bloodhounds reach us.

Father Gabriel reached into a decrepit wooden box affixed to the stone wall. "Take this. To help you and your wife on your journey to freedom." Something jingled as he passed the gift to Jean.

"Father," Jean exclaimed. "This is five crowns! We cannot accept—"

The old priest held up a hand. It shook with tremors. "That comes from the poor box. No one here now is poorer than the pair of you." He offered a crooked smile.

Still, Jean protested. "But, should we be captured and the money traced back to you—"

"Stuff and nonsense. Should the King wish me dead, I would be so. But it will be my faith for which I die, as I give you this gift in Christian charity. It will not be your fault."

Father Gabriel patted Jean, whose handsome face contorted into a look of worry. "You forget I know better than any how your conscience plagues you Jean St. Bromaine. Now go, before you too run out of time." He paused at the doorway. "And please, take the pair of white horses that came to me only this evening. You must make Dover tonight."

The Royal Forest
The Escape

"Tell me Bridget my dear." Jean spoke in low tones as the branches whipped across our faces in stinging swats. Night bugs buzzed about, some biting at our exposed flesh while others flickered harmlessly as they added what flashes of light they could to our nighttime escape. "When you were a girl, did you fancy fleeing merry ole England on the very night of your honeymoon?"

I thought back to when I was a girl at Throckenholt Priory. Skipping along the hand-laid stones, placed there by martyred monks. Burdened by a heavy guilt for being happy. For being alive. All simply by hiding my true faith—the faith of my mother—whilst living among Protestants.

Elizabeth and I had pondered often over love and marriage as young girls do, dreaming of royal weddings trimmed in purple and gold, a slave to our hearts as we gave them to only the most handsome and most rich of our suitors. All royal or of noble birth, of course.

Love? Lady Denny would scold us as though the very word was wretched on her tongue. *There cannot be love in a marriage. Love thy King, your most sovereign prince, above all. As he is the head of the Church of England and the whole of this island.*

Still, I dared to dream.

"Quite honestly Jean, no. I did no such thing." My words were quick and breathless. Jean slowed our horses' pace. "I never dreamt of a honeymoon at all, really. Lest my aunt, Lady Denny, were able to secure me to some fat, houndish groomsman for a handsome dowry price. However, that would leave me loveless, with 15 children and rotten with syphilis. All the while, my fat husband would be in the arms of his mistress, begetting bastards, and I alone with my royal misery."

Jean glanced over his shoulder. The light of laughter brightened his eyes despite the deep darkness of the forest. "It appears to me that you know the goings on at Court far too intimately."

The weight about my shoulders lightened. "Perhaps so."

The sound of crashing waves met my ears, and heavy air, thick and fresh with salt, enveloped me. My eyes fluttered open. *I must have fallen asleep.* Still, darkness surrounded me and I was strangely disoriented. "Jean?"

I mustn't have slept long.

"Jean?" My sleep-roughened voice croaked like a bullfrog.

A hand was on my knee in an instant. "I'm here, Bridget. Fear not."

My horse whuffed and stomped his hooves. I stroked his pearlish neck. "Have we made it?"

"We will leave the horses here," Jean instructed. He ignored my question as his hand skittered up my leg.

That mere touch sent waves of heat to secret places. I accepted his hand and dismounted.

"I have something to show you."

I let him lead me from the dark forest onto a moonlit beach.

"This is where the ferryman will come in the morning. Had he left his ferry, we could simply steal it and ferry ourselves to freedom. Alas, it seems he bedded down on the shores of France tonight."

I tried to still my pounding heart, but it was no use. Emotions threatened to send me over an unseen edge. Fear, desire. They mixed and brought a righteous thunder to my chest.

"Like our ferryman, we too shall bed down. Alas, we shall be here, and unbeknownst to him, it's for him that we will wait." Jean gestured toward a tinkling waterfall. "Come, Wife. Behold your honeymoon chamber."

Enchanted, I followed Jean with light steps to the bank of the river that emptied into the sea. Across a small path of stepping stones, slippery under my bare feet, and tucked just behind the curtain of water that fell from the rocky outcropping above, there it was. "Jean," I exclaimed. "It's beautiful."

The moonlight, bright off the sea, reflected through the streams of trickling water like a lantern. Cool moss tickled my feet and promised a good night's rest. However, with Jean's hands on my waist and his kisses on my neck, sleep was the furthest thing from my mind.

"Tell me you love it," he murmured into my hair. "Tell me."

I turned and let his lips trail up my neck and across the hollow of my throat, until they met mine. Gentle, yet hungry.

"I love this place," I managed through breathless kisses. "And how could I help but love you?"

With practiced hands, Jean relieved me of the cumbersome dress and lay me back onto the moss. Chill from the frigid floor of the cave crept into me, making me shiver. The look in Jean's eye told me not to worry and promised that the troublesome chill would soon be extinguished.

Joined in holy union and belonging only to each other, I let Jean lead me through the rocky foothills of pleasure, as only those with the truest of hearts can tread. I'd never dreamed of scaling any of the world's peaks, but we did so, *together*, without ever leaving our waterfall chamber.

The swishing of water against wood woke me, though the ray of sun had yet to chase away the darkness of the night. "Jean," I whispered.

Beneath my hand, his chest rose and fell with each breath. I leaned and pressed my lips to his cheek. "Jean."

The strong arm I'd been wrapped in all night curled around my waist as my husband rolled to face me, his eyes still closed. He tightened his grip, as though he was grasping a trunk of treasure on a ship that was going down. "Mmm, Bridget."

"The ferryman, Jean. I think he's arrived."

Jean's eyes opened, and a slow grin spread across his lips. "So soon? Didn't we just get to sleep?"

I flushed. Indeed, the majority of the night was spent awake, exploring, in each other's arms. A shiver coursed through my insides as Jean's fingertips traced a fiery line from my face, down my ribs, and stopped at my naked thigh.

"I suppose I should go barter with the man." Jean flashed a wink that brought a wanting ache to my core. "Wait here. And I beseech you, get dressed only if you must."

I covered my face with my hands. Jean rose, pulled on his breeches, and disappeared through the watery exit before I dared uncover them.

Ever dutiful, I stepped back into the silk dress that had spent the night crumpled in a corner. It was heavy and damp and miserable.

I may well be slipping my own noose about me neck, I thought as I worked the strings. I left the whale-bone corset on the mossy rocks that dotted the floor of our cave and stepped out from behind the veil of water.

Jean's voice drifted along the water. "Yes, both these white horses. Yours when we touch French soil."

I tiptoed across the slippery river rocks and dared a peek into the clearing. There, stood Jean and the French ferryman. The pair of white horses that had come as a blessing from Father Gabriel snorted and stomped. Something wasn't right.

The ferryman wrung his gray cap in his hands. Before he could answer Jean's offer, two guardsmen wearing the crest of Dover Castle appeared behind them. I sucked in a gasp and, careful to be silent, sneaked back into the confines of my watery hiding place.

One of the two spoke in a haughty, nasal tone. "Where are you headed so early?"

The King's men have found us.

I retreated to the far back of the cave, their voices lost in my haste. A prayer graced my lips as I squatted behind a rock. For a brief moment, I wondered if I could swim the Strait of Dover, should the need arise.

"Gown like the sky, springtime shy. Eyes like the sea, green as emeralds they be."

My eyes flew open. One of the Dover soldiers hovered at the mouth of my cave. "You're Lady Bridget." He closed the space between us in deliberate steps.

Terror shimmered in my eyes and threatened to spill onto my cheeks as I watched, helpless, as he advanced.

"Please sir, you have me mistaken—"

His gloved hand smacked over my mouth, squelching my already soft voice. "Quiet you—you—you traitorous blasphemer!"

The taste of coppery blood dotted my tongue.

"You ran out on the King, your lord. Harlot." He spat. "It is a pleasure to return you to your fate."

With his hand clamped across my mouth, he started to call out to his companion. I heard him suck in a deep breath, but the only thing that passed over his tongue and out his mouth was a thin squeak.

His hand fell from my face as he slowly sank to his knees.

Jean darkened the opening of our waterfall hideaway. As quick as he'd jabbed it, he pulled back the silver dagger, edged in the Englishman's lifeblood.

"Bridget, are you alright?"

I nodded and touched the corner of my mouth. Blood dotted my fingertips.

Jean sheathed his boot knife. "Where there is one, there is a hundred. We must make haste, my love."

I took my husband's outstretched hand and let him pull me from our honeymoon chamber. I tried not to look at the Englishman's face as I stepped over his lifeless body and back out into the thin gray dawn. The other guardsman lay in a crumpled heap at the water's edge, his red tunic made redder still by the pool of scarlet which grew beneath him.

The ferryman stood on the wooden boat, waiting. Hounds bayed in the distance. Something inside me flicked and, in that instant, and I knew that I was forever changed.

They're coming.

Grasping the tunic of the man near the water, I strained against his weight and tried to drag him to the ferry. "We can dump them in the deep waters of the channel."

"Darling," Jean's hand was light on my shoulder. "Let me." Jean grasped the dead guardsman and hefted him easily into our waterfall oasis. "We cannot link these men to our ferryman. Or they will kill him, too."

I glanced over to the man who was ready to carry us to freedom. He was feverishly kicking dirt over the pool of scarlet left by the King's man. When he was satisfied, he humphed a triumphant sound. Then, scurrying about like a rodent, he grasped the reins of the two white horses and led them onto the wooden boat. His voice trembled in dawn's early light. "If I am to take you across the channel to Calais, you must board. Now."

The wooden boat creaked as the ferryman ran it onto French soil. "Thank you God," he murmured. A sheen of sweat glistened across his forehead in the midday rays.

"I believe he is more relieved than the pair of us." Jean's voice was a whisper across my skin.

"The pair of horses had been most nervous, I would say." Relief washed over me like the frothy sea over the rocks. The King of

England's men and their bloodthirsty dogs sat safely on the far side of the sea. Their snapping barks had haunted me for miles into the open water.

Thank God I didn't have to swim.

Jean stood and pulled the ferryman to his wobbly feet. "Tell me sir, I heard tale there are peace talks in Calais with English envoys. Am I right?"

The ferryman nodded. He wrung his hat in his trembling hands at his middle.

"Splendid. Now you must take us to him."

The ferryman's mouth closed and opened, as though he was on the brink of a fit. "To, whom m'lord? You cannot mean to His Majesty—"

"Yes." Jean interrupted his blubbering and produced the jingling pouch of crowns from Father Gabriel. "Do be so kind as to lend us your horses and your time. Take us to Francis, my good man. Take us to the King of France."

It's Time
Calais, France

The castle loomed before us, ancient architecture upon ancient soil built upon hope. *My* hope.

I smoothed at my wild locks, acutely aware that I was entirely unfit to go before a king, even a French king. "I'd say this is fortuitous, King Francis just happening to be in Calais when we seek his assistance, again in Calais."

Nerves rattled my words, but still they kept coming. "Never until this moment have I set eyes on French soil. It looks rather, well, English."

Jean turned to me and tucked a lock of unruly hair behind my ear. The sound of the white horses' hooves galloping down the rocky road, away from us, gave me pause.

"But our horses—" I protested.

Jean's hand found mine. His palm was not the least bit sweaty, in stark contrast to mine. "Darling," he began in shushed tones. "They are our horses no longer. Our Ferryman earned them and more. From here, you and I must walk. For should we wander to the castle on such fine steeds such as those, Francis's men will no doubt watch us with even a warier eye."

I followed his pointed glance down at our pitiable clothing. Jean spoke the truth. While his own garments didn't need mending, they could certainly use a good wash. The blue silk gown I'd worn at Henry's palace and on my mad dash through the Royal Forest was a complete disgrace. Ripped here and there, I would be better to wear servant's rags than this royal disaster.

"It will be difficult enough to gain an audience with Francis," Jean continued, "without giving them more reason to think us suspicious, especially since neither of us carry letters of recommendation from King Henry. Should we be successful and gain an audience..."

His words trailed off to the tune of crashing waves.

"And if we are not?"

The coastal air was thick with salt and added heavy volume to my unbrushed mane. I batted it with my free hand, careful not to loosen my fingers from Jean's grip with the other. He offered yet another grim smile.

Flashes of Dudley's nubby-toothed grin and the promise of his torture chamber gave me pause. The hunger in his broken voice gnawed at my soul. When he spoke of having time with me alone upon my return, before my execution, he became a starving dog. Only through my torture would his hunger be satisfied. The gruesome nature of King Henry's chamber was known across the land and was not simply limited to the rack or the gallows.

When Mark Smeaton, the musician among the many men accused of adultery with the late Queen Anne Boleyn was examined, it was widely whispered that a knotted rope was tightened about his head in such a manner that he emerged blinded for the remainder of his short, sad life. And that wasn't even in the infamous chamber.

It seems every instrument that could be used to inflict pain was rumored to be present in his dungeon. I shivered and gripped Jean's hand tighter. Surely the French Court had an equally ravenous torturer.

"Let's not dwell on such matters."

I began to speak, but the words strangled in my throat. I was glad of it, since fear would have broken them into unrecognizable syllables anyway.

Jean brushed my cheek with his thumb. "Fret not, Wife. I will die before I'll let any harm come to you."

Carefully, we made our way up the rocky path to the castle that may well be our ultimate undoing—or our earthly salvation.

A pair of King Francis's men stepped before us as we neared the castle gate. "*Arret!*"

My breath caught in my chest and my eyes trained on the open portcullis just inside. Jean and I came to a halt, just as the soldiers commanded.

"*Indiquer votre enterprise,*" the tall one with the thick moustache ordered.

"He said state your business," I translated quietly, but Jean didn't need me to translate for him.

"*Nous avons besoin d'une rencontre avec* King Francis," Jean relayed in perfect French.

The men's identical coffee brown eyes widened. They turned slightly and began to whisper. I figured them to be brothers.

"What do you want to see the King about?" one ventured in rolling, accented English.

Jean never faltered as he slipped between languages. "We've come from the Court of His Majesty, the King of England seeking asylum."

The quiet brother nudged the other. "It's her. The next queen."

My insides knotted, and fear froze my legs. I loosened my fingers from Jean's protective grip. Terrified thoughts came in spurts.

I could run...

I began to slink backward, despite my heavy legs.

One of the soldiers reached out a hand. "Dear lady, fear not. You'll find France to be your friend. After all, anything that gives King Henry reason to fret, in turn gives our King Francis reason to rejoice."

Jean's hand found mine again. "How did you know she was the next English queen?"

"*Monsieur*, your king chose *Mademoiselle Bridgette* for his bride long, long ago."

I remembered the strange looks that passed between the fat, plumed courtiers the night they came for dinner with Lady Dennis, Elizabeth, and myself. The way they behaved as though they shared a special secret. Had Lady Denny made me party to this match long ago? If my aunt would do such a thing, was there nobody in this world I could trust?

The French soldier continued. "King Henry invited King Francis to the dinner where he would make the choice of the next queen. She would be dressed in the finest blue velvet and silk, he said, so King Francis would know her straight away, even before she herself knew."

"Alas," the other brother said, "King Francis found himself indisposed and unable to attend such an—affair."

The pair shared a musical laugh.

Perhaps they are twins, I thought. Still, the idea that His Majesty had chosen me so long ago and still proceeded with this grand, false production made me queasy.

It was all a game. A game of hearts and hope where His Majesty knew the score before the rest of us were even told the rules.

The tell-tale blue fabric may well have been worms crawling about my skin. "Sirs, perhaps you might afford me a change of clothing?"

Finally, they stepped aside. "Of course, *mademoiselle*. King Francis will guarantee your comfort during your stay, I'm sure."

"Actually," I began. My glance flitted to Jean. "It's *madam*."

"And who might you be, sir?"

Jean lifted his chin. "Since becoming a husband to a woman wanted by the King of England, I do believe I have joined the ranks of the most hated."

The brothers exchanged a look and began to laugh anew before they started through the castle gate. "This way, young lovers."

My breath left my body in a cleansing puff. Jean offered a wan smile. "Come my love. It is time."

THE FRENCH COURT
Calais

"Show the wayward travelers in!"

I clutched Jean's hand tighter as the great wooden doors to King Francis's Throne Room swung inward. People lined the walls, which were thick with tapestries, and a trumpeter announced our arrival with a hearty blast of welcome on his horn. A dozen candelabras lit the room with candlelight warmth. Smiles graced the faces of those who stared at us, no doubt wondering how these offbeat and bedraggled English wound up gracing the French Court at Calais.

My lips twitched upward as my gaze met that of some of the French women who lined the great hall. Everything about this placed exuded friendliness, and a welcoming air hung thick about the room.

A voice from the far end of the chamber silenced what little chatter there was.

"Legend tells of a pair of English travelers who appear at the French Court in need of assistance!" With one booted leg propped masterfully atop the opposite knee, Francis's grin shone from his throne like a miniature sun.

An ornate golden crown, dotted with jewels of all colors, was nestled in his mounds of black curls. Dark brows accented deep, laughing eyes. His full lips parted with a mischievous smile beneath his full, black beard and revealed two rows of gleaming white teeth.

"That's King Francis," Jean whispered. "His large, prominent nose is as much his trademark as Henry's marriages are his."

Dressed in red and gold robes that billowed out around his tall, muscular frame, the King of France had the look of a schoolboy prince playing upon his father's throne. Though he was roughly aged equal to Henry, Francis had conquered his years masterfully. This Frenchman still maintained his youthful appearance—and his wit.

"Tell me truly, could these bedraggled souls be those very travelers?" Francis did a quick motion to the tune of raucous laughter. At once, goblets of wine were pressed into our hands.

A woman's voice joined musically with Francis's. "Yes, I believe they are. What did this legend foretell, Darling?"

A young woman swept up the steps and perched on his lap before looking pointedly at Jean and me. My eyes threatened to fall out of my skull at such a bold and brazen display.

Is this the King's Throne Room or His Majesty's harem?

With auburn curls mimicking those of the King, the girl's mane danced over her shoulders and down her back. A thin silver crown attempted to tame her hair, but succeeded only in making it more wild and beautiful. Her delicate features looked faintly birdlike.

"His wife, the Queen?"

"No, I do not see the Queen." Jean didn't look at me. "That is his official mistress, Anne."

"Would you ever take a mistress?" The words burned on my tongue, and I wasn't entirely sure I wanted to know the answer. My greatest fear, that of my husband leaving me filthy with syphilis and surrounded by a dozen screaming children whilst he entertained the women of Court and beyond, tightened my throat.

Before Jean could answer, Francis dismissed Anne. The young

redhead slinked back down the stairs and disappeared into the throng of people. "Good people, tell me. In this ancient tale, do the gracious, loving French accept these foreigners into their court?"

A drunken cheer of affirmation went up from the partygoers.

"Of course we do," Francis continued. "After all…" He let the words trail out from his mouth until they fell like a death shroud over the people.

Fear danced down my backbone as I watched the effect this man had over his subjects. It was reminiscent of what aunt Lady Denny had reported from King Henry's Throne room when he needed to impress his glory and power upon a visitor.

When all mouths were silent, Francis continued through slightly slurred words. "After all, I am the inventor of this tale." He chuckled to himself at his own private joke before continuing. "And I say anything that gives my cousin King Henry VIII displeasure simply *must* be welcome in France."

He raised his glass and, at once, Court sprang back to life. Couples whirled onto the dance floor, music started up from every corner, and the jester flipped across the floor before us. Laughter and chatter filled the stone walls and, with the mood significantly lightened, this place felt almost like home. *Almost.*

Something in Francis's spiel gave me pause. *Cousin.*

Without warning, Elizabeth burst to the forefront of my mind. Was she well? Why had she betrayed my confidence? Had she done so under coercion—or worse yet, under torture?

A prayer to Our Lady, begging her favor for Elizabeth, escaped my lips in a whisper. Despite her Protestantism, Elizabeth would always be my dearest blood relation, and I would always love her as such. All my childhood memories were wrapped up in her. In losing Elizabeth, I also lost a part of myself that could never be replaced.

"Come, my love," Jean urged, effectively pulling me out of my nostalgic reverie. "The King of France has summoned us."

A plumed courtier, not as fat as his English counterpart but even more lavishly decorated, stepped in front of us before we reached Francis's throne. "His Majesty will grant you an audience in his personal study. *S'il vous plait,* follow me."

A brandy thickened voice met my ears even before I saw anybody. "Tell me *mademoiselle,* why would you wish *not* to be married to a king?"

Jean and I rounded the stone corner and there before us sat King Francis. Only the plumed courtier stopped at his side and turned to face us. "After all, am I not a king? Am I too not worthy of your affections?"

The jovial French king I'd seen outside now bore sleety eyes and a scowl. My knees turned to water as I listed backward into Jean. "Dear God, we've walked into a trap."

Jean's arm tightened around my waist, and he stepped to my side. Words were not needed to express that he would die to protect me, even if that meant the both of us meeting Our Father tonight on French soil by the hand of King Francis—or his personal executioner.

The courtier and Francis exchanged a glance, then burst into a fit of drunken laughter. After a hearty exchange at my expense, the courtier wiped the tears from his rotund cheeks. "Your Majesty, alas, you are not famous for killing your Queens. Personally, I wouldn't marry a king like Henry either!"

Jean let go a quiet chuckle in tune with Francis and the courtier, who were both doubled over and laughing as though they didn't have single a care between them. Perhaps they did not.

I dared a small smile and glanced at my husband. He offered me a wink. "I believe that we are safer here than ever we were in England."

"Here here," Francis agreed. "Indeed you are, *monsieur.* Please, forgive my jocularity. It is not often I get to entertain guests who have absconded from the country of my rival, and I must exact as much enjoyment as possible for myself. *S'il vous plait*, sit down."

Once we were seated in plush velvet chairs, Francis continued. "Now *mademoiselle*, you obviously wished not to marry my cousin and subsequently lose your head. Your desire is to live out your life in peace, no?"

I nodded. Try as I might, I couldn't help staring at his impressive nose. Instead, I tried to study our surroundings in the quaint study, but still my gaze flitted back to his nose.

Francis appeared not to notice, or was kind enough to ignore my rude stares. "Tell me, how may I be of service to you?"

"Your Majesty," Jean began, "it seems that you know our business here as much as we do."

Francis nodded. "*Oui. Mademoiselle* Bridget's story is quite clear. However, *Monsieur*, your presence proves to be a quandary."

"*Oui* Your Majesty," Jean said through a smile. The French part of his rollicking accent was further thickened as he spoke with Francis. "I am *Madame* Bridget's husband. Jean St. Bromaine. Formerly, executioner to His Royal Highness, King Henry VIII."

Francis stared at us in silence. When he spoke, I noticed at once that the jocular tone to his voice had taken leave. "Tell me, *monsieur*, that I am the brunt of a great joke so that I may laugh with you."

"No, Your Majesty. We come before you today to humbly beseech your mercy. As you know, it is at your mercy where we find ourselves presently."

Francis sucked in a deep breath and stroked his thick beard. Slowly, he let it out. "I see."

The hem of my torn dress had found its way between my fingers. I rubbed and twisted the slick fabric until Lady Denny's voice shouted in my mind. *Don't fidget, Bridget!* Ever slow, I let go of my tattered dress and clutched my hands deliberately in my lap like the true gentlewoman I was supposed to be.

"Women, you see, are one thing, *madam*. But a man who performs services for a king—this is another matter entirely." Francis's words hovered over our heads like a guillotine blade.

After an eternal silence, Francis rose to his feet. Something had clouded his eyes, but they cleared, and he offered me the familiar bright smile I'd seen in the Throne Room. His Majesty extended both his hands to me, which I accepted without hesitation. He pulled me to my feet.

"Ah, young and reckless love. There's not a man in France who could turn you away, *mademoiselle*." He looked at Jean and feigned surprise. "Oh, forgive me—*madam*."

Francis's hands tightened around my fingers, and his dark eyes pored into mine with such intensity, I wasn't sure whether to be flattered or offended. "After all, Frenchmen are led by feelings of love, are we not? You have won the mercy of the King of France, *madam*."

"T-thank you, Your Highness." I attempted a curtsy, but Francis kept my hands held fast in his.

"Jacques," he barked.

The plumed courtier appeared beside of us, but I dared not draw my gaze from Francis's. "Majesty?"

"Show our guests to their room. They are on their honeymoon, no? Give them the Ambassador Suite."

"Yes, Your Majesty."

Slowly, Francis raised my hands to his lips and brushed a kiss across each before allowing them to sink back to my sides. Jean rose from his seat and took his place beside me. I was careful not to look at him, for fear my puzzlement at Francis's display would be met with anger.

"Jacques, these are our most treasured guests. They must be treated as such." Francis bowed deeply as Jacques ushered us toward the door. "You are both welcome in my country for as long as it pleases you to stay."

"*Merci beaucoup*," Jean managed.

As we stepped out into the stone hallway, I exhaled a sharp breath. "Praise God, Jean—"

The King's voice interrupted my quiet prayer. "*Monsieur, mendicité votre pardo.* Might I have just a little word with you? Alone?"

Francis's smiling face glowered from inside his study. The cloudiness had returned to his eyes, and a strange smile tilted his lips.

"Trust I will not keep you long from your most beautiful bride."

An overwhelming sense of dread gripped my stomach as my husband stepped back into the King's study. As Jacques pushed the heavy doors closed, I stared at Jean, and he stared back, unable and unsure of what to say. The emotion behind Jean's piercing eyes mirrored mine. *Fear.*

The doors severed our eye contact as they closed with a sense of finality.

Click.

"Come, Miss." Jacques's words were heavily-accented English. "It was said by our most sovereign prince that you require the ambassador chambers. I trust you shall be quite pleased with the most exquisite accommodations in all of France."

I willed the tears not to fall as I sat on the empty canopy bed that dominated the Ambassador Suite. I'd donned the fresh nightclothes that had been laid out for me, alongside a complementary pair for Jean, and watched from my westerly window as the sun sank until it disappeared over the horizon. As darkness descended outside, I turned toward the crackling fire that illuminated the inside of the sumptuous room. The orange glow was warm, comforting. Still, I was alone.

Jacques had been correct in his assumption—I was quite pleased with the Ambassador Suite. Deep blue curtains were held back from the window by velvet bonds that matched the trim of the bedspread.

A chess table, bathed in moonlight and set for two, waited patiently for the next players, while a writing desk, complete with its own candle sconce and footrest, sat near the fireplace. An ancient trunk stood watch at the foot of the oversized bed, while the portrait of a stranger petting his dog stared down at me from the far wall. Not too large and not too small, this room proved to be most cozy. At least, it would be cozy if Jean was here to share in the candlelit space with me.

Should he come back at all.

I glanced around and noticed for the first time a handful of recessed bricks at the head of the bed. "What's this?"

Pins and needles pricked my legs when I stood, and it took a moment until I could walk. When the feeling returned to my feet, I climbed up to examine my discovery. "Well now," I mused.

I jumped at the sound of my own voice echoing off the stones. Tucked against the back wall of the recessed bricks, stood a modest wooden cross. "Why, it's some sort of a little shrine."

Though the cross was just that, a simple cross and not a holy crucifix, and there were no statues keeping it company, I knelt to my knees before it. *Perfect height.*

I did the sign of the cross.

In nominae Patris, et Fili, et Spiritus Sancti.

A fervent prayer muddled my mind as *Hail Marys* escaped my lips.

Father, please watch over my husband.

An out-of-place creak pulled me from my prayerful trance. Slowly, I turned to discover a figure illuminated by the low glow from the fire. I gasped.

"I didn't want to disturb you while you talked to the Almighty." Jean's voice was a cool splash of water on a hot summer's day. "You are even more beautiful when you pray."

I flew into his arms. "Oh, thank God. You came back to me."

"Of course I did. Had it been up to me, I would have been here much earlier." He stroked my hair. "Tell me, did they leave some of those fancy sleeping clothes for me, too?"

Ever polite and even more nervous, I pointed to where his sleeping clothes lay. "I'll turn my back," I mumbled.

Jean didn't answer, so I averted my eyes and continued. "What did the King have to speak to you about that was so important that it lasted half the night?"

Jean stepped around and joined me on my perch on the side of the bed. *Our* bed. He covered my hand with his. "King Francis had lots to say. He most enjoyed telling me, in great detail, how Henry came to choose you as his next Queen. And why he went through the trouble of hosting all the Ladies-of-Choice in such a lavish and drawn-out display."

I shifted my weight but was careful not to move my hand from under the warmth of his. "I have been curious about that myself."

"It seems Lady Denny made it known at Court that she had two relations of marrying age living in her home. She also made it known that she would stop at nothing to see one of you—either her daughter or her niece—wed the King. He apparently had chosen you instead of Elizabeth before you ever knew what was at stake."

Something soured in my stomach as I remembered the day Lady Denny dressed Elizabeth and me in our finest dresses for a party at court. "Someone was being knighted, she said, and we were to attend with her. I didn't bother asking why she wasn't there to attend the Queen, as it was her job as her Lady-in-Waiting. I just did as I was told."

Jean rubbed his thumb across the top of my hand. "Did you meet King Henry then?"

I shook my head. "No. Not that I knew of, anyway. We stayed at Court only for a moment. We didn't even get to watch the knighting ceremony. We were ushered in and ushered out just as quickly. A few weeks later, the courtiers sent word that they would be coming to dine at Throckmorton Priory, my home."

Shivers brought gooseflesh to my arms. *Henry. He was always watching. Always cunning.*

Jean let go of my hand and draped his arm around my shoulders.

"That's when he chose you. He decided that very night who would wear the blue dress, signifying his future Queen."

"Did Francis say why Henry would go through all the trouble?"

"Yes, he did," Jean began. "It was a masterful game for a bored and lusty king. He gained a beautiful new, young wife, and his subjects gained a Queen. Both were achieved in a very public way."

I nodded and tried not to feel like a fool.

Jean continued. "Also, he increased the number of ladies at court. Mistresses, if I may be so blunt. Virginal mistresses. And he intended to enjoy them all."

The same hot bile that had surged the day I found myself lost in the castle and at King Henry's command burned in my throat again. "Please Jean, tell me no more."

"May I tell you that you're beautiful? And that every moment away from you tonight was akin to a lifetime spent in the torture chamber?"

Jean's warm breath caressed my ear with his whispers and his words melted away the hurt and fear I'd been trying to ignore.

I turned to speak, to say something. Anything. Before the sounds escaped my lips, his mouth covered mine. His passion fueled deep kisses that reminded me of adventures we'd shared together behind the waterfall. A welcome tightness brought a groan to my throat as Jean's strong fingers untied my filmy blouse.

Sweet kisses from my husband's lips trailed fire down my neck. My hands cupped his stubbled face as he proceeded to explore the body he'd known so intimately only the night before. The dampness between my thighs was discovered as Jean deftly removed my billowy night pants.

"I love you," I purred, as his kisses tickled my stomach.

The last glowing log fell in the fireplace with a thunk and cast us in only the faint, silvery darkness offered by the moon.

"Oh, my Bridget," Jean breathed against the inside of my thigh. Carefully, he pressed my knees apart. I shivered with anticipation. "If only you knew how much I loved you."

His kisses explored higher as I lay back against the bedspread. "If only you knew." Jean's voice was a throaty rasp as his fingers entered me and sent a spasm through the secret places that only Jean had ever discovered. "You would never feel fear again."

I ignored his odd choice of words and closed my eyes as my husband's lips met the slippery folds of my body. His fingers played a song of pleasure inside me that only the two of us would ever know.

My breath came in jagged gasps as Jean's kisses elicited a series of sparks that threatened to choke a scream from my dry throat. Before I could summit, Jean rose up from between my knees and, illuminated in the moonlight like an earthly angel, atop me. I grasped his waiting hardness and drew him into me.

"No," he said.

I stopped and tilted my head. "No?"

"The answer to your question from earlier. No. I should never in all my days on this earth take a mistress."

Freshly impassioned, Jean drove himself into me. I let go a throaty shout. "Jean!"

With his head tilted back, my husband growled a low growl that mimicked my own. Our breath accented each other in the night's stillness as we breathed together, harder. Faster. Deeper.

With my back arched impossibly high, I took my husband into the deepest recesses of my body again and again as we rocked together in our sensual dance until the peaks of passion were again at our mercy.

"Are you asleep?" I was careful to keep my voice at a whisper, in case he was.

Jean squeezed me closer to him in our nest of fine French blankets. "No."

I'd been tracing the lines of his chest with my fingers since we'd collapsed into the sheets, both cloaked a sheen of sweat and heavy with exhaustion. Despite sleep tugging at my eyelids, restful slumber continued to elude me.

"Tell me why things were so lengthy with Francis. And so secretive."

The words rolled off Jean's tongue and sounded more French than Welsh. "King Francis is a shrewd host, Bridget. A stupid man he is not, and he will, like Henry, use everything around him to his advantage. And his personal gain."

Jean paused a moment. In the bright white offered by the moon as it emerged from behind a black cloud, I saw him turn his face away. "In exchange for our safe lodging in France, I must lead the French Army on a surprise invasion of England. And perhaps even an attack on King Henry himself."

I swallowed hard, but the lumps that appeared with Jean's words still threatened to choke me. Every woman I'd ever known who loved a soldier did so in vain, because when a husband went away to war, he never returned. "A surprise invasion?"

"Yes." He turned back to me and let his arm fall across my middle. "I'm sure you know that you mustn't breathe a word of this outside this room. On pain of death. *My* death."

I nodded and fought the tremble in my lip. "When, Jean? When shall this take place?"

"Therein lies the torture. I will not know until the day comes to depart for England. I must be ready at a moment's notice."

A lone tear tracked from the corner of my eye.

"My love, why do you cry? This is but a small and worthy price to pay to secure your safety, and mine, far from the wrath of Henry."

Somewhere in his words, hid a kernel of truth about our safety being most far from King Henry, I was certain of it. However, it remained elusive to me as I finally lost the battle to my exhaustion and drifted off to sleep.

A New Home
Pas-de-Calais, France—April 1542

The fire from the hearth lit the kitchen of our little home to a warm glow as I set the baguette on the table. The sun would be making its appearance shortly, and Jean was probably walking back from his morning wash in the creek. Despite feeling sour in the stomach, I wanted to have a fine breakfast set out for him before he left for the day.

As King Francis promised, The Crown had provided us simple accommodations in the heart of Calais. Our one-room cottage was nestled between a bakery and a candlestick maker. The smells had been delicious and savory when we moved in, however lately, everything turned my stomach on end.

As the first golden rays of sun stretched their fiery fingers into the dark sky, I dished a ladleful of last night's warmed pottage into Jean's bowl and garnished the stew with a handful of nuts. A hunk of cheese next to his baguette along with a fresh carrot, plucked from the garden that grew behind this cottage long before we arrived, completed my husband's breakfast.

I sank down upon the chair opposite Jean's breakfast, wrapped my hands around my cup of tea, and let my eyes close. A moment later, the door opened, and Jean's cheerful whistle met my ears. He kissed the top of my head and gave my shoulder a squeeze. "Good morning, beautiful wife," he purred.

Despite the rolling nausea that had become a daily occurrence, I smiled. "Good day to my handsome husband. How was the water this morning?"

"Springtime in France promises cold water." Jean took his place across from me. "The wildflowers are a sight to behold though. Perhaps when I get back from the castle tonight, you and I can take a walk together and admire them."

"I would love that." I watched as he picked up his spoon and dove into his meal.

Jean nodded and swallowed. "If you're feeling up to it, that is."

"I'm sure I will be. I tend to feel better in the afternoons." I paused a moment. "What do you do when you go to the castle every day, Jean?"

The thought of royal mistresses, their chests falling out of their tight bodices and lust brightening their cunning eyes, had given me a great deal to worry about since coming to France. Especially since Jean had grown so closed-mouthed about his daily trips to the castle. "Please tell me?"

Jean paused in his eating and stared at me. "My darling, do you not trust me?"

"I do—" I began, but a cascade of tears made it impossible to continue.

When I dared look at him again, I discovered he was staring at me with the same piercing stare that had captured my heart when we first met. "I'm so sorry—"

He cut me off. "Bridget. I haven't told you of the goings on at the castle because I haven't wanted to worry you. Life in France hasn't seemed to agree with you, and I was certain my telling you of such things would bring you nothing but heartache."

I sniffled. "Heartache? I don't understand."

Jean abandoned his breakfast and moved around to kneel

before me. "Darling. There is talk of nothing but war. I spend my days preparing for the coming invasion, the day that I return to England is drawing near; I can feel it when I am within the castle walls. A tension hangs over the French Court." He swept a wayward lock of hair out of my eyelashes and flickered a smile. "But we are safe, you and I. We are together. We can face anything, can we not?"

I nodded. "At the bakery yesterday, there was talk of the same thing. A rumor that The Holy Roman Emperor and King Henry have joined forces to invade France."

"Ahh, so word has already spread to the town." Jean's gaze softened as he brushed my cheek with his thumb. "It's no wonder that my love is so out of sorts with worry."

The sun's rays burst through our small window. Jean stood. I knew it was time for him to be on his way. "Will you be all right alone today, Bridget?"

"Yes. Yes I will."

"*Oui.*" He bent and planted an impassioned kiss on my quivering lips. "I will see you tonight, my love."

I watched from my chair as he plucked up his uneaten carrot and stuffed it into his pocket. "Be safe, Jean St. Bromaine."

"As you wish, Mrs. St. Bromaine."

I smiled despite my turbulent emotions as the love of my life trotted out of our cottage and down the road to the French castle.

As I picked up Jean's breakfast dishes, an overwhelming sense of guilt surged within me. *Why were you so ridiculous this morning, Bridget? You didn't even allow your husband to finish his breakfast before accosting him with your groundless worries.*

I scrubbed the bowl so hard that the gray water splashed out onto my simple brown dress. I'd never been very adept at sewing and this poor garment was proof of that. I tossed the innocent bowl into the cupboard and snatched up the water bucket, no longer caring if it splashed on me. After hefting it to the backdoor, I gave the bucket, water and all, a hearty fling.

Of course, it didn't go far. But I felt somewhat better as I watched it fly through the air and meet the ground of the garden with a satisfying splat. Thankfully, the bucket didn't burst.

I strode through the streets of Calais and tried to forget the fit I'd pitched at home. Tonight's bread, a barley loaf, was nestled into my damp apron as I took in the sights and smells of my new, French home.

Jean and I had been here for months, but still I felt like an outsider. My negligible handle on the French language didn't help, either. Delicious smells that wafted out of windows tickled my nose as I wound my way along the narrow rock streets. Friendly-faced strangers bid me good morning as I walked along. Despite the raging religious fanaticism that claimed Catholicism was the true religion one day before damning it as a tool of the devil the next, I again found myself at the door of a small Catholic chapel.

I'd made it a daily mission to visit this chapel since coming to live in Calais. Once, a band of angry Protestants had preceded me into the tucked-away walls of the tiny church. I walked in as they dumped Holy Water and attempted to desecrate what they could. The pungent aroma of wine hung around them like a storm cloud, and I ducked into the confessional, lest I be seen. As quick as they descended upon the quaint chapel, they were gone.

After waiting for what seemed to be an eternity, I stepped out and surveyed the damage. Aside from a river of Holy Water pooling between the stones, they'd broken off the outstretched hand of The Virgin Mary and made a general nuisance of themselves before going along their way. I discovered the hand beneath a kneeler and placed it at her feet.

"If only I could fix it, I would," I prayed. "Fix you, fix mine and Jean's predicament, and fix England and France."

I pushed the fresh memory of the Protestant routers out of my mind and stepped into the small chapel. Thankfully, everything seemed to be in order, and Our Lady's hand was back where it belonged. *At least someone had the ability to fix it.*

"Are you here for Confession, my child?"

My heart jumped into my throat. "Oh Father, forgive me. I thought I was alone."

The old, weathered priest smiled a crooked smile. Remarkably, he appeared to still have all of his teeth. He reminded me of an ancient, gnarled oak tree, and his tufts of gray hair stuck up from his head like the fur of a mangy, angered cat.

"My child, those of us who walk with God are never alone."

I found myself nodding along with him.

"Come, my child. Step into the confessional, and unburden your soul while receiving the grace of God."

I did as I was told and allowed the ancient man to close the small wooden door behind me. I knelt at the screen. A moment later, it slid open. I did the sign of the cross.

"*In nominae Patris, et Fili, et Spiritus Sancti,*" I began. "My last confession was in my home country of England, when confessing one's sin to a priest was not punishable by burning."

"Ah, I see. As it is written, *For thy sake we are killed all the day long; we are accounted as sheep for the slaughter.* I assure you, my child, your eternal soul is safe in this House of God, no matter the country you find yourself. It is your earthly body which will die someday, and neither you nor I know when that will be."

An invisible weight lifted, and my breath came a bit easier. "Yes, Father. Some things are worthy of dying for—and Our Savior is certainly the most important of those. But that brings me to my first sin. I simply don't want to die yet. In fact, I've been running from death since King Henry VIII chose me for his next Queen.

I ran. And am running still, only now I have married and put the life of my husband in danger, too."

The old priest's voice had a laughing quality when he spoke again. "Your biggest sin is that you don't wish to die? My child, that is not a sin. That simply means you are a human."

I kept my head dipped low over my clasped hands. "Perhaps my humanness brings me to my next sin. I find myself distrustful of my husband, who risked his life to bring me to the safety of France. Now, I trust him *not* as he goes on about his affairs at the castle. I fear he does just that. Goes on about affairs."

"There is no fear in love; *but perfect love casteth out fear: because fear hath torment. He that feareth is not made perfect in love.*"

I pondered these words in silence.

The priest's voice came softer through the screen. "Sometimes, women find themselves in situations in which only women can find themselves. Perhaps there is an underlying reason for your distrust. Search your heart, my child."

My words were a whisper. "I am sorry for these, and all the sins of my past."

"Now to assign penance. It is appropriate that you pray the rosary once in the morning and once at night. In pondering the Mysteries, I believe your mind will clear and allow you to see what you need to see in order to live a—long—fulfilling life for Our Savior."

The prayer of Contrition came from my lips as I fought the urge to tell Father that I didn't own a rosary anymore. Lady Denny had put my mother's away many years ago, or perhaps she'd thrown it out like garbage. I had never been quite sure. *Perhaps I can remember the rosary and do it from memory.*

"My child, through the grace of our Lord and Savior Jesus Christ, you are forgiven of your sins. Go forth and sin no more, and be quick to forgive others as He has forgiven you."

I did the sign of the cross and stepped out of the confessional.

The priest was already there. He held out his hand. A delicate rosary dangled between his gnarled fingers. "A gift for you," he said quietly.

I accepted the precious wooden beads and crucifix with emotion clogging my throat. The beads were old, probably as old as the mysterious priest himself. Some were worn so that they were no longer spherical in nature.

Before I could formulate the appropriate response of thanks, the old priest was gone.

Jean's hand caught mine as we strode along the rocky beach. The sun would be setting soon, and the pastel show that played out above the water was a miracle in itself.

"I have been bothered all day, Bridget," Jean began. "You must trust me. I am yours and you are mine."

"I agree. I hope you'll forgive my upset—"

"My darling, there is nothing to forgive. I realized that I have not been as forthcoming with information as I should be. You shouldn't have to hear of news that affects us through townsfolk gossip."

Blue-green waves, foamy and white capped, crashed onto the bank and churned as Jean stopped and pulled me close. "So I feel I must tell you the newest of the many developments now."

I stood in silence. I'd been excited to share with my husband my mysterious encounter with the nameless priest at the small Catholic chapel, and the ancient rosary he'd given me before disappearing. The old beads hung heavy in my apron as we stood together on the pebbly sand. Now, my news seemed odd and inappropriate.

"Pray tell me," I whispered.

He pressed a kiss to my forehead before continuing. "There are further upsets between King Francis, The Holy Roman Emperor Charles V, and of course, Henry VIII." The words crashed together in my mind like the waves on the shore.

"The Holy Roman Emperor has joined forces with King Henry

and together plan to invade France. English warships have already been sighted by Frenchmen crossing the Strait of Dover."

"Does that mean—"

"Yes. The rumors are true. The time has come, my love. The first fleet of soldiers, myself included, leave at dawn. Our destination is England."

Jean clutched my hands in his as another miraculous sunset played out behind him. "Bridget, there is more you should know. You must beware of Englishmen in France. Henry has most certainly sent spies over to do his reconnaissance work of the country he means to invade."

"Reconnaissance?"

Jean nodded. "When a few men are sent out to scout before a war to see what the enemy is capable of. And what their weaknesses are." He paused a moment and then continued. "And Henry is known for his ability to hold onto a grudge. I've no doubt there is still a bounty on your beautiful head, perhaps even more rich than the one previously."

I dropped his hand and did the sign of the cross.

"Forgive me, but be mindful of that, too. Religious upsets between Catholics and Protestants are all over Europe right now, and it seems that the common theme is to burn supposed Catholics as heretics first and ask questions later."

I opened my mouth to speak, but realizing I had no words, I closed it again.

Jean offered a wan smile and, with my hand in his, began walking back toward home. "Don't betray your beliefs, but don't make yourself a target."

I trailed along with him, feeling just as dark and empty as the bucket I'd flung only this morning.

The Coast
Calais, France

I hoisted my simple dress and clambered onto the pile of rocks that stood the highest, overlooking the beach of Calais. Moisture pooled in my eyes and leaked in rivulets down my cheeks. Below, the French soldiers boarded the boats. The wind whipped my hair back as white capped waves washed up from the sea. I offered a small wave to the fleet.

Then, there he was. Jean. On the deck of the warship nearest me, standing at the railing. The White Cliffs of Dover back in England peeked up over the blue in the distance. He offered a small wave in return. From here, his icy blue eyes took on the hue of the water that had brought us to safety in France.

I pushed myself onto my tiptoes, both my arms sailing wildly about my head. A smile forced its way upon my dry lips, contrary to the heaviness in my heart. Dressed in a French soldier's uniform, my prince blended in with the others. Still, I knew the curve of his shadowed face, just as I would always know it.

"Goodbye, Jean," I called into the wind. "I love you!"

Jean kissed his fingers. He held them out in my direction before placing them over his own heart, while soldiers went about performing their duties behind him.

I kissed my fingers, held them out to him, and covered my heart just as Jean did. My words wisped from my throat. "Even an ocean couldn't offer a safe escape for us, could it, my Jean?"

On deck, a trumpet blew, and the soldiers began pulling up the ramps that anchored them to the beach. Fresh tears hung from my lashes as I stared at the man who had unselfishly saved my life. And unwittingly captured my heart.

Our last conversation echoed in my mind to the tune of the crashing waves. Jean's husky voice was sweet in my ears as though his words were real, and not simply a memory.

You are safe in France, my love. For so long as it please you to stay. But in trade for our asylum, I must lead the French Army in an invasion. An invasion of England against King Henry.

As if on an afterthought, Jean turned back to face me. High above his head, he held the rosary I'd pressed into his hand the night before when I was at my darkest.

I waved again, but slipped on the mossy rocks.

When I regained my footing, Jean was no longer at the railing.

"Goodbye my love," I said to nobody. "And Godspeed."

Alone

Calais, France—July, 1542

I awoke early, covered in sweat. The humid summer morning had little to do with my frenzied emotional state. The nightmarish dreams had, instead of abating since Jean's departure, had served only to get worse with each passing day. So much so that I dreaded going to sleep at night and found myself fighting to stay awake until absolute exhaustion overtook me in the oddest of places. Sitting in the sitting room chair. Perched at the dining table. Anywhere but laying in my empty bed. Alone.

Death. Dismemberment. Torture.

War. Hate. Pain. Mutilation.

Vendetta. Prisoner. Widow.

A sense of urgency propelled me out of the house and to the coastline. I strode down the beach where I'd said my goodbye to Jean only a month before.

Something is going to happen today. I feel it in my very bones.

A flash of movement caught my eye out over the water. *A French flag!*

"The warships," I cried into the wind. "They're coming home!"

I stood on the craggy rocks, barefoot, and waited. In seemingly no time at all, the French vessels began to pull into port. Slowly, the men began to file off, some limping, and others helping their comrades.

I searched their faces from my vantage point, looking for the piercing blue eyes that haunted my dreams, be them sleeping dreams or awake dreams. More and more men ambled off, but not one turned my way. The trail of disembarking men thinned to a trickle until there was nobody else aboard.

I sniffled and swiped the tears from my hopeful eyes and started down the rocks to find someone, anyone, from which to beg some information on the whereabouts of my husband.

Finally, I caught up with a soldier who sported a notable limp. "*Monsieur, s'il vous plait, arret.*"

I was out of breath and prayed he paused long enough to speak to me. Thankfully, he turned around gave me his full attention. "*Madam.*"

I gasped at his appearance. His sullen face was bedraggled and scarred, and his eyes, which were no doubt once vibrant and full of life, were hauntingly empty.

"Tell me. What news do you bring from England?"

The man set down his kit and stared through me. "They were ready for us. We were annihilated and withdrew."

"Annihilated?"

"Out of the four ships of men who went, we are the only ones to return."

Hysteria began to rise up within me like a living thing. "Jean. Jean St. Bromaine. You must know him. Please, tell me he is with you." I bit my tongue to keep from screaming at the wounded Frenchman.

"I know him not, *Madam*. Please excuse me, the walk to home is long, and I am tired."

"*Oui*, of course. *Merci. Merci beaucoup.*"

I watched as he picked up his kit and turned away from me. Before I could think it through, I found myself half-running, half-skipping over the sharp rocks that dotted the path from the coastline to the castle. *I must speak with King Francis. He surely knows something!*

The plumed courtier, Jacques, met me at the castle gate. "*Madam* Bridget? Is that you? You look so very..." The fat man looked me up and down as though every manner he'd been taught had taken leave. "French."

I forced a smile. "I beg an audience with King Francis, *s'il vous plait.*"

"King Francis? Surely you would like to tidy yourself a bit before asking to be presented to your most sovereign prince."

"Jacques, please. It's about the failed invasion of my former country."

Jacques big eyes widened further. "How would you know such a thing?"

"I beg you, announce my presence. Ask if he'll see me. Please."

Jacques disappeared, only to reappear moments later. His normally cheery face was stoic. "*Madame* Bridget. Follow me. His Majesty will grant you an audience in his private study."

I waited alone in the stone room. It seemed an eternity before the creak of a hidden door brought me to my feet from the same velvet chair that I'd recognized at once.

Francis strode in, as puffed up and proud as I remembered him. "Ah, my dear Bridget. Hello, hello." He held out his hands to me and kissed both my cheeks as though we were old friends.

An odd emotion niggled at the back of my mind. However, my thoughts were much too busy to bother with trying to decipher it.

Francis held my arms out and took no qualms at subtlety as he let his eyes roam over my face and down my body. "Jacques, you may leave us now."

"Your Majesty?"

Francis dropped my hands and turned to his courtier. His voice came out in a vicious snap. "I said leave us!"

Jacques retreated a few steps like a whipped pup before slinking out the still-open door. Pain was evident in his words. "As you wish, Your Majesty."

"*Merci beaucoup*, Your Majesty," I started as Jacques pulled the door shut behind him. "I beg you, tell me. What has become of my husband, Jean? He didn't return with the others this morning."

Francis paced in a slow circle around me, like a predator circling his prey. The niggling thought intensified. *Danger.*

Again, I find myself the hare. Now, I have stupidly walked into the den of the most dangerous of all the bloodhounds in France. And he's hungry.

"The men who didn't come back on our one remaining ship are presumed dead, Bridget. But fear not, I've made a secret peace with the Holy Roman Emperor. Now, we two have joined forces against our common enemy and yours, King Henry VIII of England."

His hand swept my hair over my shoulder as he stopped behind me. *Run, Bridget.*

"Rest assured, that my beautiful Bridget is safe here in France. Your husband's ultimate sacrifice has ensured your citizenship shall never be questioned."

I took a step backward as he circled around in front of me.

"And you have found yourself a widow."

Something in my face must have given away my plan of escape. Before I could bolt for the door, Francis slammed me into the stone wall. He forced his knee between my legs, and a grunt escaped his lips.

"There now," he growled as he smoothed at my hair in rough swats. "You came here for a reason. You knew your husband was dead."

"No," I managed.

"Shhhh," he warned. He squeezed the sides of my face with one hand and pressed his lips to mine. "You knew I was powerless to your charms."

I tried to shake my head, but he tightened his grip on my face. The back of my head met the wall with a sickening crack.

King Francis dragged his free hand down my face and circled my throat. Slowly, his fingers began to tighten. "Tell me you want me, Bridget."

This is it. This is the day I die.

His hand tightened further around my throat until my lungs burned for air. With no warning, Francis released my neck from his death grasp. A breath of welcome air whooshed into my chest and ensured that I would continue to live. At least for this moment.

His death-dealing hand traveled down and cupped my tender breast. I squeaked as shocks of pain sparked through my chest when he squeezed.

No, I thought. *No, no, no!*

His hand continued down my body as he removed his knee from between my legs. The exploring stopped at my belly. All his pressing and grunting stopped cold as he felt the tell-tale curve with poking, prodding fingers.

"You are—you are in a family way." He stepped back as though he'd just learned that I carried the plague. Or syphilis. "Pray tell me you are not?"

"I am." These words could be the ones that cost me my head. And my life. My thoughts drifted back to the executions of Queen Catherine Howard and Lady Jane Rochford. There, on her scaffold where nothing awaited her but death and jeers from an unpleasant crowd, Queen Catherine had the wherewithal to confess her true feelings about the King, and the man she loved, Thomas Culpepper. If she could do it, so could I—damn the consequences.

I drew in a shuddering breath. "I am happy to report that I am indeed pregnant with my husband's child."

Frances spat at me. "Your child is a bastard, Bridget."

Without further fanfare, the King of France turned his back on me, his would-be-could-be mistress, and marched across his study and out the hidden door. His cape trailed him like smoke from a fire.

Jacques, the plumed courtier, appeared a moment later. "Miss, I'm to escort you from the premises. At once."

Thankfully I'm to be guided off the premises and not to the scaffold or the dungeon.

"Sir, I accept your terms." I hoped my words weren't too jolly.

He guided me almost gently to the castle gate. "Goodbye, Bridget. And good luck." With that, castle gate closed in my face. I knew my days of being welcome in France were numbered, but I as to what that number was? I had no way to tell.

The path from the castle seemed rockier than usual and more unforgiving against my bare feet. Still, I picked my way along until Calais rose up before me. I wanted to cry, but everything inside me was numb and dry. The fresh memory of the lecherous king's hands on my body and the gleam in his eye made my skin crawl. I sank down onto a patch of grass and hugged my arms across my chest.

What to do now, Bridget? Where can I go?

Not back home, the emptiness of our quaint cottage would be too much to bear today.

Jean. My sweet Jean.

I swiped the back of my hand across my nose and got to my feet. There was only one place in the entire of France I wanted to be.

The cobblestone street was eerily quiet as I stepped into the Catholic chapel. With all the upheaval between the Catholics and Protestants, there was usually some noise buzzing around the chapel, and I had come to expect it. However, the wind through the streets was the only sound.

The sanctuary was as empty as a waiting tomb. After I dipped my fingers into the Holy Water and made the sign of the cross, I waited at the back, but no old priest appeared.

Perhaps he is in the confessional.

My footsteps, as I took the few steps across the stone floor, seemed to echo in the deafening silence.

I knotted my hands over my swollen stomach. *How will I explain the reason I am without the rosary?*

The door to the confessional was cracked a bit. I peered into the darkness inside, but nobody was there. I stepped in and pulled the door closed behind me.

Hmm. That's odd.

"Good morning, Father, I'm here for a confession," I began.

No answer.

I slid open the little screen. "Father? Are you there?"

Silence met my ears.

Perhaps he is asleep. I'll go find him.

Chills coursed over my skin without cause as I opened the confessional door and stepped back out into the sanctuary. Still, I was alone in the church. With slow and deliberate steps, I crept to the priest's side of the confessional booth and gripped the handle. It sprang open at my touch, and something fell out with a sickening thud.

The priest's gnarled hand hung lifelessly from his side of the confessional booth.

My fists were at my mouth in an instant. Backing up through the empty room, I started to scream. A thin trail of blood slid down the old hand and puddled around his knotted knuckles.

"Lady Bridget."

I froze. The chills that ran rampant across my skin threatened to turn the blood in my very veins to ice.

Before I could see who greeted me by name, a bag was yanked down over my head. The rough material dug into my face and my attacker held it tight.

My arms flailed out, but met nothing. I lost my balance and tumbled to the ground. Still, someone held the bag that stayed tight on my head.

"I don't want to have to kill you like I killed that priest—but I will. So you keep quiet, and keep still."

My breath came faster in the damp darkness, and hysteria threatened to send my heart charging out of my chest like a stallion. "I—I cannot breathe."

"Keep still, and I will loosen the bag. Perhaps. Or I may suffocate you and do England a favor." A hint of familiarity in the hissing voice gave me pause.

"Who—who are you?" I asked in shaky tones.

The faceless attacker finagled with my hands until they were lashed together behind my back. "Lady Bridget, I'm returning you to England. It is high time you face your punishment for running out on your sovereign lord, King Henry VIII."

All the blood in my body seemed to curdle at once. I opened my mouth to assure him he had the wrong person, to protest, to say anything—but a swift strike to the back of my head sent my thoughts and words flittering into nothingness like shards of broken glass into the night.

The serene sound of water lapping near my head urged me awake. My head throbbed a righteous throb, and the world was still cloaked in darkness. I wiggled my fingers, which were numb and still lashed tight behind my back.

Grunt. Splash.

I listened and tried not to move.

Grunt. Splash.

Someone near me began to mumble. "Almost done now. All this time, almost done."

Father, help me. Please. Not now. Not this way.

I cleared my throat. "Begging your pardon m'lord—"

"You! You hush you—you—you wretch."

Grunt. Splash.

"I assure you, good sir, I'm no wretch. If I've offended you in some way, I am deeply sorry."

Grunt. Splash.

"You transgressed against me when you ran out on the King, His Majesty."

I blinked in the darkness of my burlap prison, but it did no good. I'd been laying down, so I struggled to sit up. The little boat lurched with my movement.

"Be still, damn you!"

"Is there still a bounty on my head?"

Grunt. But the splash didn't follow. "How did you know about that?" He laughed a nasal, snorty laugh.

So familiar. "Please, I beg you—" At once, his face popped into my mind. The plumed English courtier! He'd dined at my home, directed us from Queen Catherine's execution, and lorded over us at that wretched dinner façade. I recalled his fat belly and the way he favored his left leg—not as mightily as King Henry favored his—but he sported a definite limp. "You were so kind to me, sir. Surely you haven't bred hatred in your heart for me since we last met."

Splash. We were moving again.

"I know there was an invasion of French soldiers in England. I am glad you weren't hurt."

Something in his voice softened as he continued his struggle to row us across the water. "Aye, yes. Many were killed, including that bastard headsman. Jean St. Bromaine."

I bit my tongue until I tasted blood. Still, I refused to take the bait and incriminate my beloved. "You know, Lady Bridget, I had my suspicions about the pair of you from the beginning. What with that display at Queen Catherine's execution, and then the pair of you running out under the cover of night. However—"

Grunt. Splash.

"It was my pleasure to dispatch him. Venomous traitor that he was."

Anger boiled up within me.

"M'lord, is it the King's pleasure that I be returned to him blinded by his servant?"

"As a matter of fact, no. His Majesty says you are to come to him whole and alive."

My heart picked up speed and slapped against the inside of my chest. "Then, might you be able to adjust the blindfold? The knot is in my eye."

"Blindfold? There is no blindfold."

"Something is pressing into my eye!" I feigned a growing hysteria. "Please! Help me! I cannot feel my hands!"

With a great grunt, he started my way across the wooden boat. *Step-offstep. Step-offstep.* My heart galloped within me, and I ignored the throbbing in my head.

It's now or never.

"By Jove, you're hands have gone black." He slashed the tie that bound them, and they fell like dead weight against the wooden boards of the floor of the boat.

I tried to ignore the pain that seized them.

"Here now, let's see your eye." He leaned and began to tug at the bag. "Well, perhaps if I loosen it just a bit here—" The moment I saw a glint of daylight, I ducked my head from under the bag.

"What the—"

I squinted against the piercing rays of the sun and kicked out with both legs. Right into his paunchy gut. "Oomph!"

Father, please be with me.

I struck again, this time aiming all my attention at his bad knee. He fell heavily to the bottom of the boat. We lurched and a swell of nausea burned the back of my throat. I grabbed the side with my almost-worthless hands and vomited into the frothy water below.

From behind me, I heard him stagger to his feet. I got to mine first.

Using the momentum of the boat as it rocked, dipping so low that water sloshed over the edges, I charged. He was still wavering, in a fruitless attempt to regain his balance, when my shoulder struck him squarely in the chest. We both stumbled toward the side. His foot hit an obscure oar, and he tittered only a moment before falling into the freezing water with a noble splash.

I managed to catch myself on the side of the boat and watched as he bobbed like an elegantly tufted cork. The roasted peacock with the gilded beak came to mind, though I wasn't sure why.

His watery cries met my ears as he swirled further from the boat. "I—cannot—"

Sputtering broke his pleas into jagged fragments.

"Swim!"

Another rouge thought burst to the forefront of my mind, and with it erased everything else. My baby.

I cupped my hands round my swollen middle and dropped to my knees. Had he survived my near murder? A fringe of tears pattered the tops of my cheeks like raindrops on long-dead field. "Baby? Oh Baby..."

Kick. Won't you kick my hand?

I adjusted my fingers until they were splayed out and covering as much of my belly as possible.

Baby, where are you?

Nothing.

Something hit the side of the boat. I looked up. Through the veil of tears, I saw fingers, grasping for life.

Hail Mary full of grace. The Lord is with thee.

I grabbed the oars and began to row.

Blessed are thou amongst women.

I heard him sputtering. Alive, he meant only death for my baby. And me. The old Bridget could never have listened to a man drown mere inches from where she sat. She would have done something, anything, to wrest his life from the Reaper's grasp.

And blessed is the Fruit of Thy Womb Jesus.

"Let go!" I screamed. "You only want me dead!"

His fingers began to slip as I pulled the oars through the water.

Holy Mary, mother of God.

Pray for us sinners. Now...

Finally, his fingers slipped beneath the choppy surf.

And at the hour of our death. Amen.

A flurry of movement made my stomach lurch. "Oh thank you, thank you," I cried. "Baby, you're alive!"

I glanced over my shoulder. There was the English coast. To the front of me was France. But she offered no safer refuge for me than merry old England.

I must see for myself if Jean is gone.

I leaned forward and gave a mighty pull. The rickety wooden boat shot through the water and propelled my baby and me straight toward the English shore.

Unwelcome in England

My arms and back ached as I pulled my way through the Strait of Dover. As I neared the English coastline, the baying of hounds made an unwelcome addition to the watery percussion that throbbed against the boat. I dared a glance over my shoulder and mentally welcomed the break. Horses lined the shore.

"He had men waiting for him!" I grimaced and reset my grip on the oars. The last gurgly breaths of the courtier threatened to haunt me as I pondered over the way I'd let him die.

Could I have saved him?

Should I have given him a second chance?

Perhaps he would have taken pity on me and set me free, had I pulled him from his watery tomb.

The men that waited on the shore, with hounds and steeds, put my fears to rest. "They anticipated a fight. For me to run. And this time, they wouldn't fail in their endeavors to capture me."

I pulled hard with my right hand, and allowed my left oar to dip into the sea. *The only chance I have is to evade them on the water.* "There must be somewhere else to dock." My muscles screamed at me as I struggled to turn the tide.

Finally, I had the boat pointed away from the men. Barks and howls and whines followed. When the winds shifted, it sounded as though they were in the boat with me. Then, the winds blew them away and left silence as my only companion.

I let go of the tied-in oars and rubbed my wrists with my raw hands. My tongue was thick with thirst and being surrounded by salty sea water reminded me of an old Greek myth, but I couldn't place the title. "Surely he had water here."

I glanced around the floor of the boat. There it was! In the furthest tip. A canteen. Not wanted to capsize in this deep-sea water, I crawled across the length of the boat and grasped the canteen in my hands. In one long drink, I drained it of its contents before realizing what it was.

I spat onto the deck. "Brandy!"

The world spun a bit as I resumed my seat between the oars. I glanced about, but saw only sea. "Oh no. I fear I'm lost."

The water rose and started toward me. By the time it reached the little boat, the wave was over my head and tipped with frothy white. It slammed hard against my meager vessel and I crashed from my seat onto the floor.

Like a turtle on its back, I struggled to get up. Another wave, more massive than the first, ensured I stayed down.

Another crashed over me. Then another. I felt the creak and moan of the poor boards as they tried their best to stay together. Alas, their attempts were futile. With each wave that hammered over me, the boat came more and more deconstructed. Bit by bit. Like a child taking apart a puzzle.

Another wave crashed over me with finality and demolished the remainder of the boat. I went down, but held my breath. When I surfaced, I grabbed wildly for something, anything, to help keep me afloat.

Finally, my fingers circled around a curved and splintered board. With a prayer somewhere in my mind, I kept hold of the board as it did its job and kept me afloat while the relentless waves crashed over, under, and around me.

Seawater shot up my nose and burned with its frothy saltiness. I struggled to spit it out, but as soon as I did, more filled my mouth. *Is this what it's like to drown? Am I dying here? Today?*

Thoughts of my unborn child popped into my mind like tiny bubbles. His tiny whimpers, his bright smile. No doubt, his would mirror Jean's. He would have my stubborn will and question all that was told to him. Unless—

Unless he was a she.

She would be comfortable in all settings, be it with aristocrats or the poorest of the poor among Londoners. Beautiful would be just the beginning of words to describe her. Her personality, looks, and spirit—and still it would fail to adequately capture her essence.

Another wave pushed me down beneath the swirling surface. I flailed my arms and legs with reckless abandon, but my board of salvation was gone. A bed of rocks from the shallow sea floor jutted up and caught my leg. The blood billowed out in a scarlet veil as their knifelike edges sliced into my calf.

When the waves rolled back, I grabbed for the exposed rocks. In a welcome show of mercy, these beach rocks were round and smooth, in sharp contrast to their underwater counterparts. Like an accidentally-buried drunk emerging from a shallow grave, I pulled myself to the shore.

Barks from bloodhounds, punctuated by men's shouts, bounced off the trees and echoed all around.

Are there really that many?

I shook off a shudder and dragged myself onto the pebbly beach. Blood oozed from my leg and trailed me across the wet sand. My head still spun from the brandy and adrenaline, which made the world whirl around me.

The cover of the woods. I must get under the cover of the woods.

Finally, I reached the tree line. My leg burned and stung. I moved considerably slower than I envisioned myself moving.

Only this time, Jean isn't waiting in the woods to save me.

The barking dogs and shouting men grew nearer still. Again, I was the hopeless hare. A sharp pain in my leg made me stumble as I attempted to dash through the woods at a frighteningly slow pace. I gripped my belly and prayed for my unborn child and the man I killed to get here.

God forgive me. In Nominae Patris, et Fili, et Spiritus...

Something hit my back. Time slowed to a crawl as I fell and fell. The men's chatter and barking dogs were all around. I protected my belly, but failed to protect my head. The ground rose up, fast and hard. After a burst of golden stars, my vision went black.

I awoke to a world that was fuzzy and dark. Light entered the black through slats that sliced the light into stripes which then fell across the darkness in pale fingers.

Where am I?

Horses whinnied and stomped. A whip snapped. Men voices congealed in my head but failed to make sense. I struggled to sit up, but couldn't. The chains that bound my hands and feet clinked together and ground into my flesh.

I tried to speak, only a groan escaped. "Uhhhhhhh."

A masculine voice spoke clearly in the darkness. "Ah, The Great Escapist. You won't escape now."

My stomach churned, and I choked back nausea. "Where am I?"

He sounded as though he was chewing on something. He spat. "You're going to stand trial for treason at Dover Castle."

The iron gate ground against its hinges before they opened the back of my buggy. My captor heaved a mighty groan as he exited first. "Come on, out with you."

I allowed him to help me out, and for the first time, fully experienced the extent of my bonds. My head and leg throbbed, and my hands and feet were wrapped in chains. By Grace alone, my belly was left untouched.

Thank you, God.

"Into the dungeon with you."

Dungeon?

I squinted against the fading sunlight. Sure enough, it was everything that I envisioned in my most vivid of nightmares. And we weren't even inside yet.

A woman with hair askew and her head and hands fastened in a board, as though she was holding a fiddle before her, danced in the doorway. Her grin was akin to that which was worn by Lady Rochford. I began to wonder why she didn't simply run out the open gate, but then noticed the chain which kept her bound to the wall by her ankle.

"Once you go in, won't come out," the big man guffawed. "And remember, we're always watching."

My gaze followed the direction of his pointed finger, and I gasped. A wretched, severed head stared down at me through eyeless sockets from a spike above the gate. Long black hair concealed the gender, but the mouth was contorted in a gruesome way that must have been a scream in life.

I wrinkled my nose and tried not to show any fear as they led me into hell.

When we arrived at my cell, my captor unlocked my chains. I almost thanked them, but caught myself. Instead, I rubbed my aching wrists and glanced around at the accommodations. Nothing. Nothing except a wet mound of straw scattered in the corner and a rock privy in the corner.

I stepped over to examine it. When I lifted the lid, I was shocked to see that the hole over which one relieved herself emptied directly into the rushing river below. The momentary thought of escape, by prying some of the surrounding rocks away until one might fit through the privy hole, rushed through my mind.

You could do it, Bridget. But the fall into the river would kill you. Or kill the baby.

Peering through the hole, I tried to gauge how deep the river was.

If I hit the river bottom and failed to die, it would be the torture chamber with utmost certainty.

I eased the lid back down and exhaled. Fleeting dreams of escape rushed on down the river to their demise. My eyelids fluttered and exhaustion thankfully overtook me as I stumbled across the floor to my makeshift bed. Happy to be alive, I slept soundly with the rats in my very own mound of rotting straw.

The next day dawned dismal. At least, I assumed it was dawn. Seeing as how I had no window, the gentle rays of sun failed to awaken me. It was the moaning howls and terrified shrieks of my dungeon-mates that did their job instead. I pulled my aching frame from the pile of hay.

My leg had stiffened considerably overnight, and the crust of blood had proven to be a delicious snack to my furry cellmates. Fresh trails streaked scarlet down my leg and onto my bare foot. I hobbled to the door and pushed myself onto my tiptoes.

A pair of King Henry's men, armed with steel blades and covered in armor, strode purposefully down the dank hall toward me, then slowed as they approached my cell.

"The traitor wench goes on trial this morning. We'll take her the long way, through the torture chamber."

I jumped back against the wall. My pulse drummed in my ears. They were coming for me.

"**B**ridget, you should have tried escaping through the privy," I admonished myself as the iron keys jangled in the lock. My hands, still sore and slightly discolored from being bound in the boat, trembled as I clutched my baby in my belly. We would have had a fighting chance that way. Now, we are as good as dead.

A growl came from the other side of the splintery door. "Dammit Langston, you're still drunk. That's the wrong key."

Tears burned in the back of my throat. "I miss you, Jean. God be with you, beloved husband, wherever you are."

A rogue thought burst to the forefront of my mind. The ancient rosary that the priest had gifted to me. Was it clutched in Jean's hand in death somewhere on enemy English soil? Had his murderer stolen it and, being a heretic Protestant, desecrated it? Or, had his murderer been a Catholic and kept it for their own family? Had it even made the journey with him across the Strait? How I wish I had it now.

Without thought or preparation, I sank to my knees, eyes shut, despite the stabbing pain in my leg. All my worry about not remembering the sacred prayers of the rosary, the cornerstone of the faith of my mother, was for naught.

I imagined the beads in my hand, lending comfort and a divine peace to those forsaken and forgotten. Like me. The Apostle's Creed rolled off my tongue, as sweet as honey.

I believe in God the Father, Almighty, Maker of Heaven and Earth ...

"Damn it to hell, give me those keys. I'll open the door." One of the mystery voices oomphed, as though they'd been hit in the stomach. Keys jangled and I listened as the iron bolt slid out of the lock.

"Ow, Lyde." The other voice grumbled. "It makes no sense to make such a fuss over a stupid wench so early in the morning. I would much rather be sleeping."

"Sleeping it off, you mean."

I clutched my belly and smiled as my baby kicked my hands. The door slammed open, and I heard men's boots stomp into my dank cell. Rats squeaked and skittered back into the pile of rotten straw.

And in Jesus Christ his only begotten Son our Lord...

"On your feet, traitorous wretch."

I opened my eyes. Fear didn't consume me as I feared it would. Despite my smiling at him, the shorter of my two captors drew back his booted foot.

If he kicks the baby, the baby will die. I squeezed my eyes closed and curled around my stomach. An instant later, the whoosh of his swinging foot blew my hair. The squeak of the rat he stomped shrieked in my ears. On a normal day, I would cry over the rat. Today, I said a mental prayer of thanks.

Who was conceived of the Holy Ghost and born of the Virgin Mary...

I allowed them to pull me to my feet. "Now, the time has come to take your medicine. Walk now; walk faster!"

The clanking of their swords didn't deter my spirit. I smiled despite of everything that had transpired. Even when the tips of their swords touched my back, the troublesome niggle of fear did not return. No matter the cost, no matter the way I came to meet Our Lord, I'd stayed true to my faith and didn't marry a man for station or riches. I'd found love with Jean. We'd created a baby that I felt kicking within my belly. I could meet my Savior with a clean conscience and, with a little luck, Jean would be there waiting for me.

A woman's howl from an unseen cell made me shiver. I remembered the woman, chained to the wall with her hands clasped in "the fiddle." Perhaps it was her who made the noise? It spoke of agony, torment, and loneliness. Fear and hopelessness resonated in the long monotone cry, as well. What was her transgression?

Suffered under Pontius Pilate, was crucified, died, and was buried.

"There now, that way." The hallway branched. Down the lighted path were more cells and windows. Down the other—only darkness.

I turned and looked at the bigger of the two men. His sword touched my neck. Nothing on his chiseled, shadowed face bespoke friendliness.

"Which way, sir?"

He held the sword steady at my neck. His meaning was clear. He could dispatch me in a moment. I was completely at his mercy. Finally, he moved the tip of his blade and pointed into the darkness.

"There's no light?"

"Down the stairs."

"To the torture chamber," the drunker of the pair added.

I chewed the inside of my cheek and nodded. The screams of those stuck in torment in their cells that lined the lighted hall echoed behind me as I glanced into the darkness.

I sucked in a deep breath and allowed my gaze to meet that of the taller guard. His face softened a scooch. "Careful, mind you. They be mighty steep."

"Thank you." My voice was a whisper. The wall was chilly and damp as I felt for a hand rail, but found none. I took one step, then another, careful to keep one hand on the wall and the other on my protruding stomach—my first steps on the walk no one ever returned from. Surprisingly, no more swords poked me as we descended the gloomy staircase, and no harsh voices rushed me.

When we reached the bottom, darkness shrouded us completely. The larger of my captors banged on the door in sharp succession.

Almost instantly, the door scraped open. A wart-faced man wearing a deranged smile stood to greet us.

"Aye, Lady Bridget. Welcome to His Majesty's torture chamber of Dover Castle."

He descended into hell...

Behind him, sobs and whimpers from various contraptions filled the dimly lit room, stuffy with putrid odors and the faint scent of rotting death. A sorrowful excuse for a human hung in chains from the wall and moaned a low, guttural moan while another person who looked to be closer to death than life whimpered from the rack. From the ceiling hung a cage that looked like something a bird might live in, only this cage held a human. A woman with long, stringy hair and empty eyes.

Her legs hung over the side and a pained look contorted her sallow face. A fat man with a handful of feathers stood below her cage. He looked at me, then up at her bare foot. A sadistic grin spread his thin lips wide. He raised his handful of feathers and brushed them along the bottom of her bare foot. She groaned as she jerked to get away, as though the touch to the bottom of her foot was painful, only then did I see that she was tied. Upon closer inspection, the bottom of her foot looked like raw meat.

My stomach turned to think of how long she'd been there, forced to endure tickle torture. *What could her crime be?*

"You go sit there." One of the men gestured to a wooden chair at the far end of the room. "Since you're on trial, that's where you will stay until told to do otherwise."

Our Father, who art in Heaven, hallowed be thy name...

I dragged my stiff leg behind me as I walked the length of the room. Jeers rose up from the crowd on either side of me. Men, all men. Someone threw a carrot at me, but it missed. The tomato, however, splattered against my shoulder.

Thy kingdom come. Thy will be done, on earth as it is in Heaven.
Please, do your will today, Father.

"Do you know why you're here, young lady?" A severe judge stared down at me from beneath a fiercely powered wig as I took my seat.

"Treason!" The word echoed about the room as it was shouted over and over again by men who came to watch me suffer. "High Treason to the Crown!"

I looked up at the unsmiling judge. "I believe I am here because some believe I have committed treason."

"You *have* committed treason. Now tell me. How did you escape from His Majesty's castle?"

I glanced out at the sea of faces that glared back at me. Not one look of hope, not one look of sympathy. Hungry wolves, all of them. Only through my torment would they be fulfilled, but only temporarily. Once my suffering and humiliation were over, they would become miserable yet again.

Lady Rochford flickered to my mind, her smiling face on the day of her execution as she smiled down at me. It was all so clear now. She had been searching for any ounce of kindness, any friend amid a surfeit of foe. Something deep inside me wished she were here today, staring up at me, as I was on trial for the very crime that cost her the most precious of all things: her life. Treason.

"Answer, damn you!"

Hail Mary, full of grace. The Lord is with thee.
Be with me, too.

"I walked out of the castle gate."

"Did nobody try and stop you?"

"Nobody was able to stop me."

The judge addressed the bickering crowd. "Who helped you? Surely a stupid woman couldn't have escaped from His Royal Highness's castle without some sort of assistance?"

"Escaped?" I didn't have to feign shock. "I was told I was a guest. I did not realize that I was His Majesty's prisoner."

A clever lawyer could have run amok with my words, alas, no lawyer was appointed to help me. Instead, the judge simply ignored me.

"Tell the Court of your dealings with Jean."

"Jean?"

Pray for us sinners, now and at the hour of our death. Amen.

The rapping of a gavel against wood brought the chittering courtroom back to an obedient silence. "Jean St. Bromaine. The servant of His Majesty that coincidently went missing the same night as His Majesty's future wife! You!"

"Does that mean this Jean of which you speak was also a prisoner of His Majesty without knowing it?"

The judge stammered in a response but wound up closing his mouth instead.

So I continued. "Did this Jean know that he was not supposed to leave? And are you entirely certain he left and it wasn't some tragedy that befell him instead?"

The judge's eyes grew wide.

"Perhaps someone should search for him instead of—"

"Enough!" The judge's voice climbed an octave and I feared his red face might send him into a heart seizure. "Who do you think you are to tell me anything about anyone at any time!"

He banged the gavel righteously, like a madman, until his face was a light purple in color. "Order, order, order! For God's sake!"

When he finished his fit, his wig sat askew, and his wide eyes were punctuated with small, red dots on the whites of them. "Take her away, men! Back to London where she will be rightly and justly *executed* for *treason*."

Some faceless voice spoke up. "She appears to be with child. Can one be executed in such a condition?"

The judge snorted louder. "Any woman who would abdicate her duties to marry King Henry VIII is dually noted to be insane. As we know, following the execution of Lady Rochford, it is now legal to execute insane women."

He glared down at me with hate hot in his eyes. "As for that bastard she carries. Her womb was designated and divinely chosen for use by the King himself and none other. This truth alone shows that, beyond the shadow of a doubt, the heathen bastard occupying the traitor's womb is also guilty of High Treason!"

An uneasy silence cloaked the courtroom as the judge sat on the bench, snorting like an angry bull, just waiting for provocation to explode again. After a moment, a man in the back gingerly raised his hand. "Why not execute her here? And be done with the likes of her?"

That bit of provocation was all he needed. "The traitor's execution will be carried out in London, where His Majesty may attend if it be his pleasure!"

I bit my lip and my throat threatened to close. My hands tightened around my unborn child, the living remembrance of my beautiful, perfect husband. It was done and over and scarcely anyone had cared for what I had to say, aside from the sour judge. Then, my words only angered him more, and effectively made me into more of an enemy. I sucked in a breath. I wouldn't let them execute me or my child without fighting to the last breath.

The judge banged his gavel again. "Take her to London, men, as it pleases the King."

And now, a sneak peek at

HIGH TREASON
The King's Pleasure ∾ *Book 2*

HIGHWAYMEN

Guilty. High Treason. Back to London. That unborn bastard is guilty, too. As it pleases the King. The words were a fog, blotting out all my senses. Except one. The only feeling that remained was a sense of absolute and total dread. My baby, conceived in love with my husband Jean before he was forced by King Francis to wage war for France on our native England, fluttered in my stomach.

"Take the traitor—and her bastard—to London," the sullen-eyed judge hissed. "And may God have mercy on your soul. If He so chooses."

The larger of my two captors strode toward me, a length of chain stretched before him. He kept his voice a whisper as he approached. "Come now, Miss."

I pushed my aching frame up from the unforgiving wooden chair, to the jeers of the crowd, and accepted the chain. My lower lip trembled as he draped the iron links across my protruding belly.

He clipped my hands into the shackles, but didn't tighten the chain. "Don't fret, Miss. I'll take care not to make it too tight."

"T-thank you." The tremble in my lip moved to my voice.

"I'm Lyge, Lady Bridget. Allow me to escort you to the carriage."

"Not to the dungeon?"

He shook his head. "Perhaps a prayer will calm your nerves, m'lady?" Lyge matched his steps to mine as we strode the length of the courtroom. "I noticed it kept you on your feet on the walk here."

I dared a glance at him. Still unsmiling, his face was somehow softer. Kinder.

"Most people put on trial for treason pass out when Ramish opens the dungeon door. You, however, did not." Lyge pushed on the wooden door leading out of the castle. A whoosh of fresh air and sunshine welcomed us. If not for my chains, I might have smiled. "You would have made a fine queen, Lady Bridget."

Horse hooves clomped along the stone street. I knew the black carriage they pulled in an instant. My stomach turned over as it ground to a halt in front of us. "Thank you for your kindness, Lyge."

"My sister was chosen as a Lady-of-Choice."

My eyes widened as the doors on the back of the carriage flung open. "Really?"

"Seems she had an occurrence with her lapel dipping into her soup bowl. She said you were kind to her. For that, I thank you, Lady Bridget."

He bowed his head, as I stood, dumbfounded.

"Come on with you," a guttural voice barked. "Road to London shan't get any shorter."

"Godspeed, Lady Bridget," Lyge whispered as he helped me into the back of the carriage. "And God's will be done."

The doors slammed shut and closed me in the stuffy darkness of the carriage. It may as well have been a tomb.

A hand clasped over my bare ankle. "He didn't properly secure you," the man growled. His fingers dug into my flesh.

I whimpered. "I am secured, sir." I balled my bound hands into fists, but nothing much could be done to protect myself, or my baby, should the need arise to do so.

Slowly, the man dragged his fingers up my leg.

"Please stop," I begged.

"Now, there's nothing to do between now and London. But I can think of a few things."

I shook my head, but it was useless. He couldn't see me in the absolute darkness. "No," I shouted.

His hand met my cheek with a smack before falling back into my lap. At once, they began to fumble with my dress.

The carriage jerked to an abrupt halt. A voice, presumably our driver's, called out a greeting. "How may we be of assistance?"

Silence filled the tense air as my carriage-mate contained to fumble with my dress.

"I say hello there," the driver tried again.

Brusque words answered the unasked question as to why we stopped. "This is a holdup."

"No use holding us up," the driver retorted. "We're transporting a prisoner to London for further interrogation and subsequent execution."

Interrogation. Dudley's stumpy smile filled my mind. The royal torturer would finally be granted his wish.

I batted at the probing and unwelcome hands that seemed content to do as they wished despite my refusal and tried to scoot away.

A holdup?

I sucked in a breath. This may be my only chance. "Help me, please!"

The lecherous man smacked his hand over my mouth. "Shut up, wench," he seethed.

"Open the door." The metallic sound of steel being unsheathed met my ears. "Now."

Keys jingled, and a moment later the doors sprang open. A masked highwayman wielding a curved blade stood domineeringly behind the driver.

"What are you doing, man?" The driver's brow knitted together over his eyes. "You're back here to ensure she doesn't escape. Not have your way with her."

"She's going to die, mate. May as well have my way with her. Say, why do you—"

The masked men stepped forward and yanked him from on top of me. In an instant, the man who couldn't keep his hands to himself was on his knees behind the carriage. Without any last words or any more conversation, the masked man held his blade aloft and brought it down in a swift swipe. The would-be rapist's head fell to the ground. I gasped.

The masked man shifted his gaze to me and his piercing blue eyes threatened to burn right through me. I recognized them at once.

"I'll take the prisoner into my care," he declared. "She'll be my hostage."

The gruff words, a mixture of French and Welsh, were sweet as salvation. The driver unlocked my chains and helped me out of the carriage as the life-saving highwayman dragged the corpse of the headless man into the woods.

"Go driver," he commanded, once the scene was normal again. "Tell them, if you must, that she escaped. Again."

I stood there, next to him as the carriage rolled down the street and turned around a bend. Out of sight.

At once, the highwayman took me into his arms. "Jean!"

"My darling Bridget," he breathed into my hair.

Only then did I realize I was shaking.

"Come, we haven't much time." His hand caught mine. I let him lead me into the thick woods until an outcropping of ruins jabbed at the horizon. "We'll bed down here."

Together, we picked through the rubble until we found a place to sit.

"Your timing," I panted, "is impeccable."

Jean swiped the mask from his face. A smattering of scars bespoke of torment in the days we'd been apart. A smile tilted his lips upward. "So you said on our wedding night."

A rabid flush burned my neck and crept into my cheeks. "But how did you find me?"

"I was there. At your trial."

Shock furrowed my brow. "How?" *And how did I not see you?*

"My darling, now that we are out of France and the mission is complete, I can tell you the rest of the truth."

I sat up straighter.

"Since the day we arrived in France seeking refuge, King Francis had other plans for me."

"He had you lead the invasion. Of England." My voice grew meek. "Right?"

Jean nodded. His hand found mine. "I was a mercenary spy for France since day one. Telling you that would have put you in grave danger."

I took a moment to process the news. "Francis would tell you nothing, when you inquired about me to him, would he?"

"He would not," I agreed.

"The coach driver," Jean continued, "was also on the elite squad of mercenaries who worked with me to get you out of Henry's clutches.

"Not the man in the back with me though."

Jean shook his head. "I don't know where he came from." He sat in silence a moment. "But, the pair of us should be fine. If we get out of England now."

The new revelations swirled around me, confounding me, like the Word of God, no doubt boggled the mind of a nonbeliever.

The questions as to where we would go, what we would do, how we would manage—they fizzled into nothing as my baby leapt and kicked within me. I licked my lips. "Did you stay for the entire trial, my love?"

"No. Long enough to see that you were safe, is all. Once you were there, everyone knew the outcome and what it would be. So I left straight away to make arrangements for your release." He smiled. "Er, should I say your capture."

"In that case, I have news, too." I took my husband's hand and placed it on my middle.

Seeming to sense Daddy was near, the baby fluttered even more. Jean's handsome face paled.

"I'm pregnant."

Sara Harris and her family have made their home in places all over the world, from the majestic Oklahoma plains to the eclectic mountains of Italy—collecting inspiration and rescue animals along the way.

Sara is a member of the Romance Writers of America, Critique Chair of RWA's Hearts Through History group, Western Fiction-eers, West Houston Romance Writers, The Catholic Writer's Guild, and The Transylvanian Society of Dracula.

Sara, her romance novel-esque husband, and their children make their home in Katy, Texas. She has her BA in Medieval European History and is represented by Julie Gwinn of The Seymour Agency.

Connect with Sara online at:

www.SaraHarrisBooks.com

Also Available From

S ARA H ARRIS

House of Madness
Katie's Plain Regret